		DATE DUE	

Breast Cancer

Peggy J. Parks

Diseases and Disorders

ReferencePoint Press®

San Diego, CA

© 2014 ReferencePoint Press, Inc.
Printed in the United States

For more information, contact:
ReferencePoint Press, Inc.
PO Box 27779
San Diego, CA 92198
www.ReferencePointPress.com

Picture credits:
Cover: Dreamstime and iStockphoto.com
Maury Aaseng: 30–32, 44–46, 58–60, 72–74
©A. Ariani/Splash News/Corbis: 17
©BSIP/Corbis: 15

LIBRARY OF CONGRESS CATALOGING-IN-PUBLICATION DATA

Parks, Peggy J., 1951–
    Breast cancer / by Peggy J. Parks.
        pages cm. -- (Compact research series)
    Audience: 9 to 12.
    Includes bibliographical references and index.
    ISBN-13: 978-1-60152-548-2 (hardback)
    ISBN-10: 1-60152-548-6 (hardback)
 1. Breast--Cancer--Juvenile literature. 2. Oncology--Juvenile literature. I. Title.
    RC280.B8P293 2014
    616.99'449--dc23

                                                                        2013028194

Contents

Foreword

As modern civilization continues to evolve, its ability to create, store, distribute, and access information expands exponentially. The explosion of information from all media continues to increase at a phenomenal rate. By 2020 some experts predict the worldwide information base will double every seventy-three days. While access to diverse sources of information and perspectives is paramount to any democratic society, information alone cannot help people gain knowledge and understanding. Information must be organized and presented clearly and succinctly in order to be understood. The challenge in the digital age becomes not the creation of information, but how best to sort, organize, enhance, and present information.

ReferencePoint Press developed the *Compact Research* series with this challenge of the information age in mind. More than any other subject area today, researching current issues can yield vast, diverse, and unqualified information that can be intimidating and overwhelming for even the most advanced and motivated researcher. The *Compact Research* series offers a compact, relevant, intelligent, and conveniently organized collection of information covering a variety of current topics ranging from illegal immigration and deforestation to diseases such as anorexia and meningitis.

The series focuses on three types of information: objective single-author narratives, opinion-based primary source quotations, and facts and statistics. The clearly written objective narratives provide context and reliable background information. Primary source quotes are carefully selected and cited, exposing the reader to differing points of view, and facts and statistics sections aid the reader in evaluating perspectives. Presenting these key types of information creates a richer, more balanced learning experience.

For better understanding and convenience, the series enhances information by organizing it into narrower topics and adding design features that make it easy for a reader to identify desired content. For example, in *Compact Research: Illegal Immigration*, a chapter covering the economic impact of illegal immigration has an objective narrative explaining the various ways the economy is impacted, a balanced section of numerous primary source quotes on the topic, followed by facts and full-color illustrations to encourage evaluation of contrasting perspectives.

The ancient Roman philosopher Lucius Annaeus Seneca wrote, "It is quality rather than quantity that matters." More than just a collection of content, the *Compact Research* series is simply committed to creating, finding, organizing, and presenting the most relevant and appropriate amount of information on a current topic in a user-friendly style that invites, intrigues, and fosters understanding.

Breast Cancer at a Glance

What Breast Cancer Is

Breast cancer develops when cells in breast tissue become abnormal and start growing out of control.

Common Types

The two most common types of breast cancer are ductal carcinoma and lobular carcinoma, both of which may be *in situ* (nonspreading) or invasive.

Uncommon Breast Cancers

Two types that are less common than others, as well as especially aggressive, are inflammatory breast cancer and triple-negative breast cancer.

Breast Cancer Stages

Physicians define breast cancer in terms of stages 0 through IV, which indicate whether the cancer has spread and the patient's chances of survival for five years.

Prevalence

Worldwide, breast cancer is the most common type of cancer among women, with an estimated 1.6 million new cases occurring each year.

Warning Signs

The most common symptoms of breast cancer are a lump in the breast or changes in breast size or shape. There may also be changes in the nipple, such as a leaking of blood-tinged fluid.

Causes

Scientists do not know what causes most breast cancers, although obesity, alcohol use, and radiation treatment to the chest are believed to increase risk. From 5 to 10 percent of breast cancer cases are linked to abnormal genes.

Diagnosis

Diagnostic mammograms, ultrasounds, and magnetic resonance imaging can help diagnose breast cancer, but only a biopsy can absolutely confirm it.

Treatment Options

Most breast cancer patients undergo some type of surgery, often combined with chemotherapy and/or radiation treatments. Hormone therapy may also be used.

Success Rate of Treatment

Breast cancer mortality rates have decreased 27 percent since 1990, which many cancer experts attribute to better treatments.

Prevention

Nothing is guaranteed to prevent breast cancer, but eating a healthy diet, keeping weight under control, avoiding alcohol, and exercising regularly can help lower one's risk.

Overview

❝'Your biopsy was positive for breast cancer.' These are among the most terrifying words a woman can hear from her doctor. Breast cancer elicits so many fears, including those relating to death, surgery, loss of body image, and loss of sexuality.❞

—Jerry R. Balentine, chief medical officer and executive vice president of St. Barnabas Hospital and Healthcare System in the Bronx area of New York City.

❝Breast cancer survival rates have increased, and the number of deaths has been declining, thanks to a number of factors such as earlier detection, new treatments, and a better understanding of the disease.❞

—Mayo Clinic, a world-renowned health-care facility that is dedicated to patient care, education, and research.

Vanessa Bell Calloway is a veteran actress of stage, television, and film. She has appeared in the Broadway production of *Dreamgirls*, movies such as *Coming to America* and *What's Love Got to Do with It?*, and the TV series *Shameless*. Throughout her adult life Calloway has been diligent about taking care of herself and maintaining a healthy lifestyle. Much of her motivation has been career-related, as she explains: "Because I'm an actress, being fit goes along with the job description."[1] In 2009, however, she learned that even with the most steadfast commitment to health and fitness, some things are just not within her control.

Calloway was fifty-one years old when she received a disturbing phone call from her doctor after having a routine mammogram. "I heard the dreaded words no woman wants to hear," she says. "The results of my mammogram were 'suspicious.' In my mind I knew 'suspicious' could mean cancer, but as much as I tried not to dwell on that reality, I somehow couldn't stop myself."[2] Calloway's worst fears were confirmed when a biopsy, which is a sample of tissue taken from the body to examine it more closely, showed that she had cancer in her left breast.

Agonizing Choices

Once Calloway got past the shock of the diagnosis, she was motivated to move forward with treatment and put the nightmare behind her. Rather than undergo a mastectomy (removal of her entire breast) she opted to have a lumpectomy. With this procedure, only the tumor and a margin of surrounding tissue are removed, leaving most of the breast intact. After the operation, Calloway assumed that her battle with breast cancer was over—but she was wrong. Diagnostic scans showed that some cancerous tissue remained in her breast, so she underwent a second lumpectomy. When that operation also failed to eliminate all traces of cancer, she accepted that her only option was to have her left breast removed.

> " The severity of breast cancer is defined in terms of stages, which indicate whether it has spread within the breast and/or to other parts of the body. "

Four years have passed since Calloway's mastectomy, and she has remained cancer-free. In that time, she has seen one daughter graduate from high school and another daughter graduate from college. "I plan on being present to witness much more in the years to come," she says. Still, the shadow of what she went through is always there, hovering in the back of her mind: "It's never very far away from me that I am a breast cancer survivor."[3]

When Cells Go Awry

To understand the disease of breast cancer, it helps to know what cells are, how they normally behave, and how they can change. Cells make up all living things. The human body is composed of trillions of different types of cells, all of which miraculously work together to keep people healthy. These cells continuously grow and divide in a controlled way. In a natural renewal process known as apoptosis (or programmed cell death), cells that grow old or become damaged die and are replaced with new cells.

But sometimes, for reasons that scientists do not understand, this process does not work the way it should. The genetic material (deoxyribonucleic acid, or DNA) of a cell changes or becomes damaged, which is known as a genetic mutation. This affects normal cell growth and division so instead of dying, old or damaged cells begin growing out of control to form abnormal cells—cancerous cells. Breast cancer experts Carey K. Anders and Nancy U. Lin explain: "Cancer cells that arise from, for instance, breast tissue, grow and divide out of control; they also become undifferentiated, which means they lose the distinguishing characteristics of the original tissue, (i.e., normal breast)."[4] Unlike normal cells, those that turn cancerous have the ability to spread to distant regions of the body, which is known as metastasis.

What Is Breast Cancer?

Like all types of cancer, breast cancer develops because of uncontrolled cell growth. Although it can begin in any part of the breast, it most often originates in the cells of the ducts. These are described in Johns Hopkins Medicine's overview of the female breast:

> Each breast has 15 to 20 sections, called lobes, that are arranged like the petals of a daisy. Each lobe has many smaller lobules, which end in dozens of tiny bulbs that can produce milk. The lobes, lobules, and bulbs are all linked by thin tubes called ducts. These ducts lead to the nipple in the center of a dark area of skin called the areola. Fat fills the spaces between lobules and ducts.[5]

The severity of breast cancer is defined in terms of stages, which indicate whether it has spread within the breast and/or to other parts of the body. Breast cancer stages range from 0 to IV, with many subcategories in between. Lower numbers are indicative of earlier stages of cancer; higher numbers reflect cancer in later stages. Stage 0 breast cancer, for instance, is very small and noninvasive, whereas stage IV has spread extensively, most often into the lungs, bones, liver, or brain.

Staging is also an indication of relative survival rates, which compare the survival of breast cancer patients with that of people in the general population. "For example," says the breast cancer organization Susan G. Komen for the Cure, "the five-year relative survival for stage II breast cancer is 86 percent. This means women with stage II breast cancer are, on average, 86 percent as likely as women in the general population to live five years beyond their diagnosis."[6]

Types of Breast Cancer

Researchers have identified a variety of different breast cancers. The specific type that someone has depends on which cells turn cancerous and where in the breast the cancer originates. The most common type is ductal carcinoma, which begins in the cells that line the milk ducts in the breast. The two subtypes are ductal carcinoma in situ, in which the cancerous cells remain in the lining of the ducts and have not spread to other tissue; and invasive ductal carcinoma, in which the cells have broken through the ducts and spread into other parts of the breast tissue and/or other parts of the body. According to Johns Hopkins Medicine, invasive ductal carcinoma constitutes about 80 percent of all breast cancer diagnoses and is the most common form of breast cancer.

Lobular carcinoma, which originates in the lobes or lobules of the breast, is also a common type of breast cancer. As with ductal carcinoma, lobular carcinoma may either be in situ (nonspreading) or invasive. According to the National Cancer Institute (NCI), lobular carcinoma tends to develop in both breasts more often than other types of breast cancer.

> **One of the most typical warning signs is a breast lump.**

One particularly aggressive type is inflammatory breast cancer, which develops when cancer cells block lymph vessels in the skin of the breast. It is particularly rare, constituting only about 1 to 3 percent of all breast cancers. It is called "inflammatory" because the breast looks like it is inflamed, meaning swollen and red, as the American Cancer Society writes: "Usually there is no single lump or tumor. Instead, inflammatory breast cancer . . . makes the skin on the breast look red and feel warm. It also may give the breast skin a thick, pitted appearance that looks a lot like an orange peel."[7]

Another aggressive form of breast cancer, known as triple-negative, is not as rare as the inflammatory type but still only comprises 5 to 10 percent of breast cancer cases. Triple-negative breast cancer is related to the absence of receptors, which are proteins found inside and on the surface of cells that control functions such as cell growth and death. Breastcancer.org explains: "These receptor proteins are the 'eyes' and 'ears' of the cells, receiving messages from substances in the bloodstream and then telling the cells what to do."[8] Many types of breast cancer are fueled by receptors for the hormones estrogen and progesterone, as well as for the substance known as human epidermal growth factor. In women with triple-negative breast cancer, however, all three types of receptors are missing. Because many treatments are designed to target these receptors, triple-negative breast cancer is often challenging to treat.

Breast Cancer Prevalence

The American Cancer Society defines *prevalence* as "the number of living people who have ever had a cancer diagnosis."[9] This includes people who have been diagnosed with cancer in the past as well those who were recently diagnosed. The group notes that as of February 2013, there were more than 2.9 million breast cancer survivors in the United States. Nearly 70 percent of breast cancer cases affect women aged forty-five to seventy-four, with the average age at diagnosis about sixty years. Although males can develop breast cancer, it is about one hundred times more prevalent in women.

> " Even though scientists are aware that out-of-control cell growth leads to cancer, they do not know *why* this happens. "

The highest overall incidence of breast cancer is among Caucasian women, followed by African American, Hispanic, Asian/Pacific Islander, and American Indian/Alaska Native women (in that order). Some types of breast cancer, however, disproportionately affect particular groups of women. Triple-negative breast cancer, for instance, is more common among African American and Hispanic females than Caucasian females. It is also

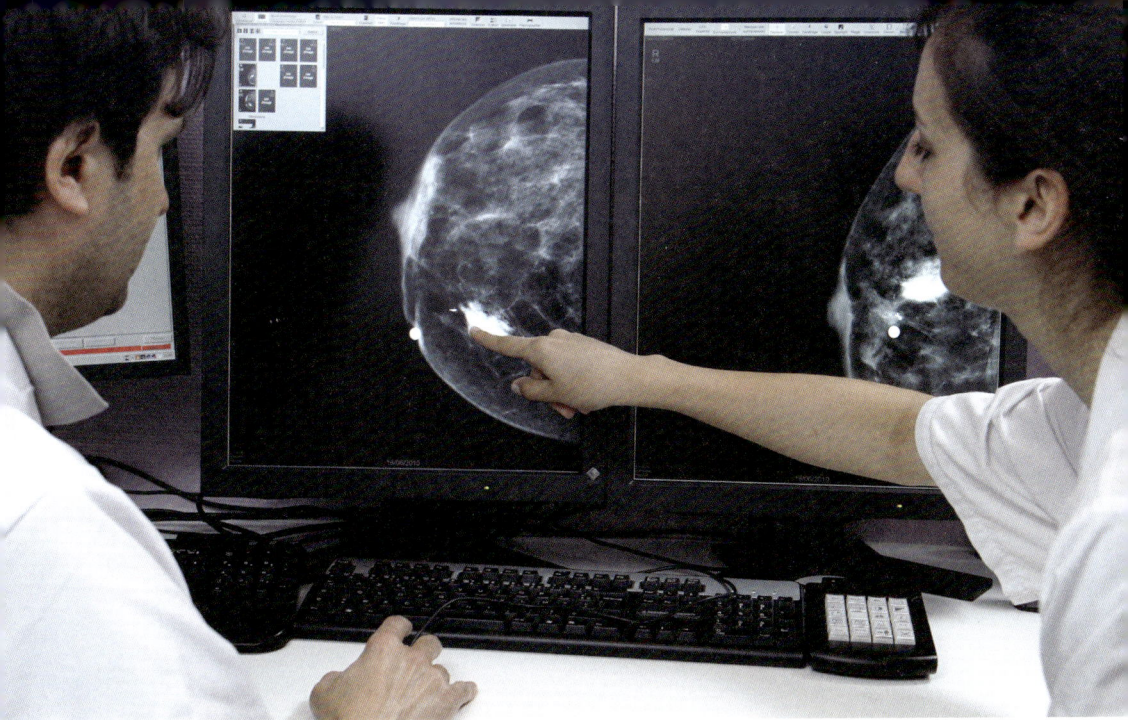

Technicians review an image of a patient's breast and a spot that might be breast cancer. Doctors usually take tissue samples, called biopsies, to determine whether suspicious growths are cancerous.

more common among Ashkenazi Jews, or Jewish people who trace their roots to central or eastern Europe.

Warning Signs

No two breast cancer patients are exactly the same, but there are some common signs and symptoms that could indicate the presence of breast cancer. One of the most typical warning signs is a breast lump. Or someone may notice changes in the size or shape of a breast. Other possible symptoms involve the nipple, such as peeling, scaling, or flaking of skin, or the leakage of fluid (other than milk), especially if it is blood tinged.

Those with rarer types of breast cancer may experience some unusual symptoms. This was the case with Holly Newman, a thirty-four-year-old wife and mother from Lincoln Park, Michigan, who noticed what she refers to as bizarre symptoms. "The first symptom was my nipple inverted," she says, "and then my breast swelled up and turned bright red. It was very hot, very painful."[10] Initially, doctors thought that Newman had some sort of infection, but tests later showed that she had inflammatory breast cancer.

What Causes Breast Cancer?

Even though scientists are aware that out-of-control cell growth leads to cancer, they do not know *why* this happens. Even after decades of research, precisely why some people develop breast cancer when so many others do not remains a mystery. Risk factors that are suspected of increasing someone's chance of developing the disease include treatment with radiation therapy to the breast or chest during childhood or adolescence, obesity, and drinking alcohol. Another risk factor is taking the hormones estrogen or progesterone for symptoms of menopause, the period during a woman's forties or fifties when her menstrual cycle ceases.

Certain types of breast cancer are known to be linked to genetic mutations, although this applies to only about 5 to 10 percent of all breast cancer cases. Most of these are related to abnormalities in two genes: BRCA1 (BReast CAncer gene 1) and BRCA2 (BReast CAncer gene 2). These genes perform essential functions in the human body, such as ensuring the stability of cellular DNA and helping to prevent uncontrolled cell growth. The Fred Hutchinson Cancer Research Center explains: "The BRCA1 and BRCA2 genes are part of the body's normal mechanism to fix mistakes that occur in the DNA when cells go through normal division."[11]

When either BRCA gene has a mutation, however, it loses its ability to perform properly and increases susceptibility to breast and ovarian cancer. For example, the average woman in the United States has about a 12 percent lifetime risk of developing breast cancer. Comparatively, women with a mutated BRCA1 or BRCA2 gene have a lifetime risk as high as 85 percent.

How Breast Cancer Is Diagnosed

If someone finds a suspicious lump or has other reasons to suspect breast cancer, a variety of tests may be used to confirm the diagnosis. The first step is usually a clinical breast exam, during which a health-care provider checks both breasts to feel for any lumps or abnormalities. The American Cancer Society explains: "Special attention will be given to the shape and texture of the breasts, location of any lumps, and whether such lumps are attached to the skin or to deeper tissues. The area under both arms will also be examined."[12]

Additional tests, such as magnetic resonance imaging (MRI), will follow the clinical breast exam. The MRI creates high-quality images and is especially useful at locating hard-to-find cancers. An ultrasound can also help diagnose breast cancer. With this technology, high-energy sound waves bounce off internal tissues or organs and make echoes, forming a picture called a sonogram. A technician examines the sonogram to look for areas that appear suspicious.

Another test that may be used is a diagnostic mammogram. This involves the same basic technology as a routine screening mammogram, but more images are taken to focus on the area of concern. A diagnostic mammogram can have varying results, such as showing that an abnormality is not worrisome at all, that an area of abnormal tissue is likely benign (not cancerous), or that the abnormal area is suspicious enough to warrant further testing.

> " If someone finds a suspicious lump or has other reasons to suspect breast cancer, a variety of tests may be used to confirm the diagnosis. "

For a breast cancer diagnosis to be confirmed, a biopsy must be performed. One widely used type of biopsy is the fine-needle aspiration biopsy, in which a very thin, hollow needle attached to a syringe is used by the doctor to withdraw (aspirate) a small amount of tissue from the problem area of the breast. A pathologist examines the sample under a microscope to check for the presence of cancer.

Treatment Options

Treatment varies depending on the type of breast cancer, how advanced it is, the patient's overall health, and his or her personal preference. According to the Mayo Clinic, most breast cancer patients have some type of surgery in addition to chemotherapy, hormone therapy, and/or radiation.

Chemotherapy is a treatment that uses drugs to destroy cancer cells. It often begins as a follow-up treatment to surgery, but patients with larger tumors may be treated with chemotherapy before surgery. The Mayo Clinic explains: "The goal is to shrink a tumor to a size that makes it easier to remove with surgery."[13] Radiation therapy uses high-powered beams of energy (such as X-rays) to kill cancer cells and/or keep them from growing.

This treatment may be done by using a large machine that aims the beams directly at the site of the patient's cancer or by placing radioactive material inside the body.

Patients who have a type of breast cancer that is sensitive to hormones may benefit from hormone therapy, which the Mayo Clinic says is "perhaps more properly termed hormone-blocking therapy." This treatment helps prevent hormones such as estrogen and progesterone from fueling the growth of breast cancer, and it can involve taking drugs by mouth or intravenously. The Mayo Clinic writes: "Hormone therapy can be used after surgery or other treatments to decrease the chance of [the] cancer returning. If the cancer has already spread, hormone therapy may shrink and control it."[14]

> " **Chemotherapy is a treatment that uses drugs to destroy cancer cells.** "

How Successful Are Breast Cancer Treatments?

To evaluate the success (or failure) of breast cancer treatments, experts compare statistics from the past with current data—and the news is promising. Studies show that death rates from breast cancer have steadily declined over the years: In 1950 the five-year survival rate for breast cancer was about 60 percent, compared with an average of more than 90 percent today. "Many breast cancer survivors are now celebrating 10, 20, 30 or more years of being 'cancer-free,'" says the National Breast Cancer Coalition, "which is certainly a cause for celebration. Breast cancer mortality rates have actually decreased 27 percent from 1990 to 2005. Although no one knows the exact cause of the decrease, many attribute it to the introduction of better treatments."[15]

Despite this progress, breast cancer is still a killer. It remains the leading cause of death among women worldwide, and according to government reports, it claims nearly forty thousand lives each year in the United States. And even though the survival rate has markedly improved, the term *cancer-free* is not necessarily the same as *cured*. The National Breast Cancer Coalition writes: "We do have more treatment options and more targeted therapy, but we don't understand the disease well enough to know for certain which cancers will come back and/or spread, and which

Actress Angelina Jolie announced in 2013 that she had undergone a preventive double mastectomy after learning that she had a heightened risk of developing breast cancer. Jolie's announcement focused world attention on breast cancer and on preventive measures chosen by some women.

cancers will not. And we cannot tell any individual woman at the end of her treatment that she is 'cured.' We just do not know."[16]

Can Breast Cancer Be Prevented?

Because scientists are not sure what causes breast cancer, there is no absolute way to prevent it from developing. People can, however, take steps to reduce their risk, such as eating a healthy, low-fat diet that is rich in fruits and vegetables; keeping their weight under control; being physically active; avoiding alcohol; and for women, limiting postmenopausal hormone therapy.

According to the NCI, clinical trials that focus on breast cancer prevention are under way in many parts of the United States. Some of these trials are conducted with healthy people who have an increased risk for developing breast cancer. Others are conducted with participants who have had cancer and are trying to prevent a recurrence or to lower their chance of developing another type of cancer. Clinical trials may also help determine whether actions people take can help to prevent cancer. The NCI writes: "These may include exercising more or quitting smoking or taking certain medicines, vitamins, minerals, or food supplements."[17]

In some instances, women who test positive for a BRCA gene mutation and who have a history of breast cancer in their families have taken a more extreme approach to prevention. They have undergone preventive mastectomies. This option came to public attention in May 2013 in an article written for the *New York Times* by actress Angelina Jolie. In the article Jolie announced that she had undergone a preventive double mastectomy despite no sign of cancer in either breast. She made this decision, she wrote, because genetic tests showed that she carried a mutated BRCA gene and because breast cancer runs in her family.

Progress and Challenges

Breast cancer is a disease that develops in breast tissue as the result of abnormal cells, although how and why cells turn cancerous is a mystery. Even after decades of study, researchers still have as many questions as answers. They have made progress, however, in terms of expanded scientific understanding and better treatments, which has led to improved quality of life as well as higher life expectancies. In the future, research may yield discoveries that finally produce a breast cancer cure.

What Is Breast Cancer?

> **Breast cancer remains the most feared disease of all women, regardless of age, race, ethnicity, or culture.**
>
> —Lillie Shockney, a breast cancer survivor who is a University Distinguished Service Assistant Professor of Breast Cancer and administrative director of the Johns Hopkins Breast Center.

> **Breast cancer takes a tremendous toll on women and men of all ages, races, and ethnicities, as well as on their families and communities.**
>
> —Interagency Breast Cancer & Environmental Research Coordinating Committee, an advisory group composed of scientists, advocacy organizations, and representatives of the federal government.

Awareness of breast cancer is widespread today, with the iconic pink ribbon among the most famous and recognizable symbols in the world. But there was a time when breast cancer was considered a taboo subject that was rarely, if ever, discussed publicly. That began to change in the fall of 1974. First Lady Betty Ford revealed that she suffered from breast cancer and had undergone an operation known as a radical mastectomy, during which both of her breasts were removed. Women throughout the country were empowered by what she did, as her daughter, Susan Ford Bales, explains: "Mom bluntly said the time for women hiding this disease in shame behind closed doors has to stop. And by golly, who better to make that happen than the first lady of the United States? Mom decided the public should know exactly—and I mean, exactly—what was happening to her. In an instant, Betty Ford rendered a public service that changed the history of women's health forever."[18]

A Promise Fulfilled

One woman who was inspired by Ford's willingness to speak out was Nancy G. Brinker of Dallas, Texas. Three years after Ford's announcement, Brinker's sister, Susan G. Komen, was diagnosed with breast cancer. Treatment kept it in check for a while, but the cancer was aggressive and eventually spread throughout her body. Komen accepted that she was going to die, and before she did, Brinker promised that she would do everything in her power to put an end to breast cancer.

Two years after Komen's death, Brinker created the Susan G. Komen Foundation in her memory. One of the first people she reached out to was Betty Ford, who graciously agreed to help with the organization's launch. Brinker writes: "Working elbow to elbow with our earliest volunteers . . . Mrs. Ford was pivotal in helping us launch a crusade that has changed the world for millions of breast cancer survivors and their families."[19]

An Invasive Disease

When someone dies after a battle with breast cancer, it is because the cancer has metastasized, or spread to another part of the body. The Metastatic Breast Cancer Network explains: "No one dies from breast cancer that remains in the breast. Metastasis occurs when cancerous cells travel to a vital organ and that is what threatens life."[20] Unlike noninvasive cancers, metastatic cancer is not contained within a tumor or in nearby tissue. Rather, cancer cells have broken away from the point where the cancer originated, traveled to other parts of the body, and started growing there to form secondary cancers.

> **There was a time when breast cancer was considered a taboo subject that was rarely, if ever, discussed publicly.**

Cancer can spread in several different ways, such as sending "fingers" of cancerous cells into normal tissue surrounding a tumor. It also spreads through blood, as the British group Cancer Research UK writes: "When it is in the bloodstream, it is swept along by the circulating blood until it gets stuck somewhere, usually in a very small blood vessel called a capillary. Then it must move back through the wall of the capillary and into the tissue of the organ close by. There it must start to multiply to grow a new tumour."[21]

Another way cancer spreads is through the lymphatic system, which is composed of lymph vessels and lymph nodes. Lymph vessels are thin tubes that carry a clear, watery fluid called lymph. These vessels lead to lymph nodes, which are small, bean-shaped structures that act as filters for the lymphatic system and also store white blood cells that fight infection. Clusters of lymph nodes are found in the armpit (axillary lymph nodes), above the collarbone, and in the chest, as well as in other parts of the body. When cancer spreads via the lymphatic system, it is very similar to how it spreads through blood, as Cancer Research UK

> " Cancer can spread in several different ways, such as sending 'fingers' of cancerous cells into normal tissue surrounding a tumor. "

explains: "The cancer cell must become detached from the primary tumour. Then it travels in the circulating lymph fluid until it gets stuck in the small channels inside a lymph node. There it begins to grow into a secondary cancer."[22]

Breast Cancer Stages

Breast cancer staging indicates how serious a cancer is (including whether it has spread) and the patient's relative chances of surviving for five years. To determine a patient's breast cancer stage, doctors consider the size of the tumor, whether cancer cells have spread to axillary lymph nodes, and whether the cells have spread beyond that point to other locations in the body. In situ breast cancers, for instance, are classified as stage 0, which some health-care professionals refer to as "precancer." Because cells are abnormal, though, and have the potential to become cancerous, stage 0 cancer is generally considered an early form of cancer.

Stage I breast cancer is still at an early phase in which the tumor is small: no more than 2 centimeters (just under ¾ inch), with cancerous cells contained within the breast. If the tumor begins to spread into the axillary lymph nodes, it has progressed to stage II. The cancer may also be considered stage II if it has not spread into the lymph nodes but the tumor has grown larger than 5 centimeters (2 inches).

Stage III breast cancer is divided into three subcategories: III-A, III-B, and III-C. According to the Mayo Clinic, stage III breast cancer has not yet spread to distant parts of the body, but it has steadily worsened, with the tumor increasing in size. By stage III-C, the cancer has spread to ten or more axillary lymph nodes. Stage III-B or III-C cancer that has spread to the skin of the breast may be inflammatory breast cancer.

When cancer has spread outside the breast and lymph nodes into other parts of the body such as the brain, lungs, liver, and/or bones, it has progressed to stage IV. At this phase the cancer is very advanced and the prognosis is not good. One woman who was diagnosed in 2011 with stage IV breast cancer was Kay Campbell, who founded a group called METAvivor for people with stage IV breast cancer. When asked how she copes with the possibility of death being so close at hand, Campbell offers a feisty reply: "Let's get this straight: Neither you nor I know when we are going to die. I just happen to have a diagnosis that comes with a death certificate—not yet filled in."[23]

Rare and Vicious

The word *inflammation* refers to changes in body tissue that often result from injury, irritation, or infection. An inflamed area typically becomes reddened, warm, and swollen, which is caused by increased blood flow and the buildup of white blood cells. Inflammatory breast cancer (IBC) fits this description because its symptoms are similar: The breast area swells and becomes warm and red. But, says the American Cancer Society, "this does not mean that IBC (or its symptoms) is caused by infection or injury. The symptoms of IBC are caused by cancer cells blocking lymph vessels in the skin."[24]

IBC differs from more prevalent types of breast cancer in several important ways, such as the absence of

> " When cancer has spread outside the breast and lymph nodes into other parts of the body such as the brain, lungs, liver, and/or bones, it has progressed to stage IV. "

obvious symptoms. Unlike the breast lump that is characteristic of most breast cancers, there is no lump with IBC. This presents diagnostic challenges, as the American Cancer Society explains: "Because it doesn't look like a typical breast cancer, it can be harder to diagnose."[25] This proved to be true for Renee Dillon, a woman from Syracuse, New York. While vacationing in the Bahamas in August 2012, she noticed that one of her breasts was tender and felt harder than the other one. By the time Dillon got home a week later, her breast had swelled up and was red and warm. She went to her gynecologist, who diagnosed her with a breast infection known as mastitis and prescribed antibiotics to treat the condition.

> **According to the American Cancer Society, the lifetime breast cancer risk for men is about one in one thousand, compared with one in eight for women.**

After several rounds of antibiotics, Dillon's breast showed no signs of improvement, so another doctor ordered an ultrasound. It showed that she had a mass in her breast, which a follow-up biopsy found to be cancerous. The doctor was totally baffled by her symptoms. This is not at all uncommon according to Beth Overmoyer, who directs the IBC program at Dana-Farber Cancer Institute in Boston, Massachusetts. She says that most doctors are not familiar with inflammatory breast cancer, as she explains: "Because it is so rare, not every oncologist [cancer specialist] or surgeon has good experience with the disease and one needs to understand the nuances of this cancer."[26] Dillon started doing her own research, and from what she found, she became convinced that she had IBC. Even though a physician she consulted disagreed, Dillon was convinced that she was right—and she was.

Dillon visited the Dana-Farber Cancer Institute, where tests confirmed the diagnosis of IBC. To her dismay, a biopsy also showed that her cancer had progressed to stage IV. "What would have happened," Dillon asks, "had I not been proactive enough for my own health and not gone there?"[27] As of June 2013 she was undergoing aggressive treatment for her breast cancer and vowed to keep fighting it.

Young Victims

A known fact about breast cancer is that the likelihood of developing it increases sharply as people get older. The average age is about sixty, with fewer than 1 percent of all breast cancer cases occurring before age thirty. Yet the disease does affect younger women. Because this happens so infrequently, those who develop it often feel alone and isolated, as George Sledge, a medical oncologist at Indiana University Simon Cancer Center, explains: "There's no time at which breast cancer is a fun disease to have, but it can be [awful] in the youngest group of women."[28]

Lisa Osterman was only thirty-one when she was diagnosed with breast cancer, and she soon found that none of her friends could relate to her feelings or fears. "For me it's a very isolating experience," she says. "When older women are diagnosed with breast cancer, they have a girl-friend, cousin, or sister who has had that experience. . . . But when a young woman is diagnosed with breast cancer they only know older women."[29] Osterman was fortunate to find a support and advocacy group called the Young Survival Coalition, which was created especially for young women with breast cancer. She has continued to stay involved with the group even though treatment has brought her cancer under control.

Breast Cancer in Men

Osterman's experience with feeling isolated is not unique to young women. It is also an unfortunate fact of life for men with breast cancer, because the disease so rarely affects males. According to the American Cancer Society, the lifetime breast cancer risk for men is about one in one thousand, compared with one in eight for women. And since men are often unaware that they can develop the disease, they typically do not seek medical attention at an early stage, such as when they first notice a lump or other abnormality. As a result, male breast cancer is often not diagnosed until later stages.

In the case of Thomas Sword, the problem was not that he waited too long to get a breast lump checked—it was that his doctor's office did not take him seriously. He called and was told to have it checked in about three weeks, but he insisted on being seen that same day. After his breast cancer diagnosis was confirmed, Sword endured discrimination most everywhere he turned, including from his boss, his insurance company, a physician, and a college professor. "Support for males with breast cancer? No," says Sword. "Support from doctors? No again. Support from Susan Komen Foundation? No. I cannot get people to understand how we force men with breast cancer into the 'shadow of pink' because we become insignificant. . . . Breast cancer does not discriminate. Unfortunately our society does."[30]

A Lingering Threat

A great deal has changed since 1974 when Betty Ford publicly revealed that she had breast cancer. Awareness has soared over the years, and this has helped save lives—but breast cancer has not gone away. Despite the progress that has been made, it remains a deadly disease. As scientists continue to explore breast cancer and broaden their knowledge, perhaps the day will come when people talk about it only in the past tense.

What Is Breast Cancer?

66 **Breast cancer is a random and deadly disease.** 99

—Susan G. Komen for the Cure, "Breast Cancer Facts," August 2012. http://ww5.komen.org.

Susan G. Komen for the Cure is the world's largest grassroots network of breast cancer survivors and activists.

66 **Breast cancer is no longer viewed as one disease, but rather a group of diseases under the umbrella of 'breast cancer.'** 99

—Carey K. Anders and Nancy U. Lin, *100 Questions and Answers About Triple Negative Breast Cancer*. Burlington, MA: Jones & Bartlett, 2012.

Anders is a clinician-scientist and an assistant professor of medicine at the University of North Carolina, and Lin is a medical oncologist in the Department of Medical Oncology at the Dana-Farber Cancer Institute.

* Editor's Note: While the definition of a primary source can be narrowly or broadly defined, for the purposes of Compact Research, a primary source consists of: 1) results of original research presented by an organization or researcher; 2) eyewitness accounts of events, personal experience, or work experience; 3) first-person editorials offering pundits' opinions; 4) government officials presenting political plans and/or policies; 5) representatives of organizations presenting testimony or policy.

❝Breast cancer is sometimes found after symptoms appear, but many women with early breast cancer have no symptoms.❞

—American Cancer Society, "How Is Breast Cancer Diagnosed?," February 26, 2013. www.cancer.org.

The American Cancer Society is a nationwide, community-based voluntary health organization that is dedicated to eliminating cancer as a major health problem.

❝Breast cancer is not a single disease. There are many types of breast cancer, and they may have vastly different implications.❞

—Jerry R. Balentine, "Breast Cancer," MedicineNet, September 26, 2012. www.medicinenet.com.

Balentine is chief medical officer and executive vice president of St. Barnabas Hospital and Healthcare System in the Bronx area of New York City.

❝While many women go to their doctor after finding a lump, they should also be aware of any other changes to the breast or nipple.❞

—Cancer Treatment Centers of America, "Breast Cancer Symptoms," 2013. www.cancercenter.com.

Cancer Treatment Centers of America is a national network of hospitals focusing on complex and advanced-stage cancer.

❝Breast cancer cells can spread by breaking away from a breast tumor. They can travel through blood vessels or lymph vessels to reach other parts of the body.❞

—National Cancer Institute, "What You Need to Know About Breast Cancer," September 26, 2012. www.cancer.gov.

The NCI is the federal government's principal agency for cancer research and training.

66 **Men carry a higher mortality than women do, primarily because awareness among men is less and they are less likely to assume a lump is breast cancer, which can cause a delay in seeking treatment.** 99

—National Breast Cancer Foundation, "Breast Cancer Myths," 2012. www.nationalbreastcancer.org.

The National Breast Cancer Foundation's mission is to save lives by increasing awareness of breast cancer through education and by providing mammograms for those in need.

66 **Love, life, myself. I thought I knew the meaning of these words both separately and collectively until two other words became part of my life unexpectedly— breast cancer.** 99

—Lisa Ross, in "More Stories of Hope from Breast Cancer Survivors," *St. Louis (MO) Post-Dispatch*, June 20, 2012. www.stltoday.com.

Ross is a breast cancer survivor from Glendale, Missouri.

66 **Doctors used to think that breast cancer in men was a more severe disease than in women, but it now seems that for comparably advanced breast cancers, men and women have similar outcomes.** 99

—Cleveland Clinic Breast Center, *Breast Cancer Treatment Guide*, 2012. http://my.clevelandclinic.org.

The Cleveland Clinic Breast Center provides patient care for the screening, diagnosis, and treatment of all medical and cosmetic breast problems.

What Is Breast Cancer?

- The Mayo Clinic states that with the exception of skin cancers, breast cancer is the most **frequently diagnosed** cancer in women.

- According to the American Cancer Society, about one in eight (**12 percent**) of women in the United States will develop breast cancer during their lifetime.

- According to the Dr. Susan Love Research Foundation, **280,000** women in the United States were diagnosed with breast cancer in 2012.

- Based on statistics from the NCI, **6 percent** of women will develop cancer of the breast between their fiftieth and seventieth birthdays.

- According to the organization Susan G. Komen for the Cure, **every nineteen seconds** a case of breast cancer is diagnosed somewhere in the world.

- The National Breast Cancer Foundation states that only about **20 percent** of all breast tumors are cancerous.

- According to the Memorial Sloan-Kettering Cancer Center, the average woman in the United States today has a **12.6 percent** (about one in eight) chance of developing breast cancer by the time she reaches her eighties.

Global Breast Cancer Prevalence

According to the World Cancer Research Fund, an estimated 1.4 million new cases of breast cancer are diagnosed worldwide each year. Although it is the number-one cancer among women in the United States, this graph shows that nineteen countries have a higher prevalence of the disease.

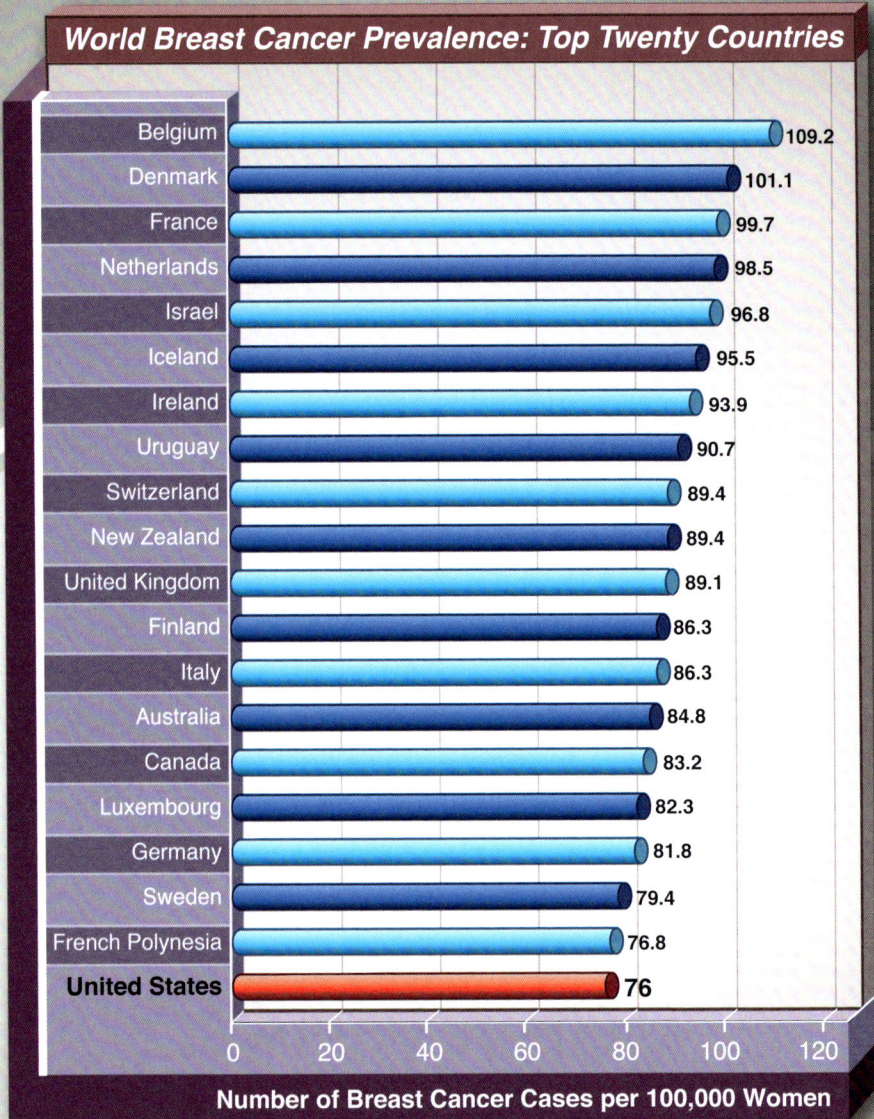

World Breast Cancer Prevalence: Top Twenty Countries

Country	Number of Breast Cancer Cases per 100,000 Women
Belgium	109.2
Denmark	101.1
France	99.7
Netherlands	98.5
Israel	96.8
Iceland	95.5
Ireland	93.9
Uruguay	90.7
Switzerland	89.4
New Zealand	89.4
United Kingdom	89.1
Finland	86.3
Italy	86.3
Australia	84.8
Canada	83.2
Luxembourg	82.3
Germany	81.8
Sweden	79.4
French Polynesia	76.8
United States	76

Number of Breast Cancer Cases per 100,000 Women

Source: World Cancer Research Fund, "World Cancer Statistics: Breast Cancer," September 2012. www.wcrf-uk.org.

Breast Cancer Warning Signs

The symptoms of breast cancer are not the same for all women, but there are some typical warning signs. Some of the most common are shown here.

☐	A breast lump or thickening that feels different from the surrounding tissue
☐	Bloody discharge from the nipple
☐	Change in the size or shape of a breast
☐	Changes to the skin over the breast, such as dimpling
☐	Inverted nipple
☐	Peeling, scaling, or flaking of the nipple or breast skin
☐	Redness or pitting of the skin over the breast, similar to the skin of an orange

Source: Mayo Clinic, "Breast Cancer: Symptoms," May 22, 2013. www.mayoclinic.com.

- According to November 2012 NCI data, from 2006 to 2010 the median age at diagnosis for breast cancer was **sixty-one**.

- The American Cancer Society says that in the United States, breast cancer is the **second leading cause of cancer death** among women, surpassed only by lung cancer.

- According to the Mayo Clinic, breast cancer most often begins with the cells in the **milk-producing ducts**.

The Most Common Cancer Among Women

According to the American Cancer Society, women are affected by breast cancer more often than any other type of cancer. This chart shows how the prevalence of the disease compares with other cancers that affect women.

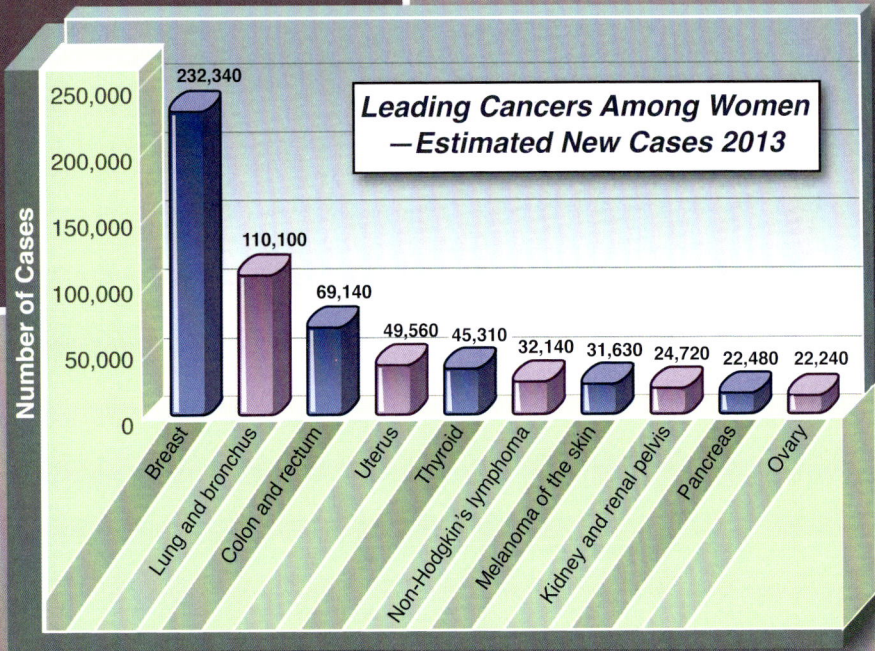

Leading Cancers Among Women —Estimated New Cases 2013

Number of Cases

Cancer	Number of Cases
Breast	232,340
Lung and bronchus	110,100
Colon and rectum	69,140
Uterus	49,560
Thyroid	45,310
Non-Hodgkin's lymphoma	32,140
Melanoma of the skin	31,630
Kidney and renal pelvis	24,720
Pancreas	22,480
Ovary	22,240

Source: American Cancer Society, "Cancer Facts & Figures 2013," January 17, 2013. www.cancer.org.

- Cancer Treatment Centers of America states that **inflammatory breast cancer** tends to occur at a younger age than other, more common forms of breast cancer.

- According to the Centers for Disease Control and Prevention (CDC), **white women** have the highest rate of breast cancer, followed by black, Hispanic, Asian/Pacific Islander, and American Indian/Alaska Native women.

What Causes Breast Cancer?

66 The causes of breast cancer remain a mystery, with a few exceptions. 99

—Lillie Shockney, a breast cancer survivor who is a University Distinguished Service Assistant Professor of Breast Cancer and administrative director of the Johns Hopkins Breast Center.

66 Although we have learned a lot, we still do not understand what causes breast cancer to develop at a certain time in a certain person. It's likely a combination of risk factors (many of which are still unknown). 99

—Susan G. Komen for the Cure, the world's largest grassroots network of breast cancer survivors and activists.

A s scientists have studied breast cancer over the years, they have posited numerous theories about what causes it. One known contributor is genetics, but that alone cannot explain breast cancer. Only about 5 to 10 percent of cases are inherited, so other factors obviously come into play. Many scientists are convinced that the disease is linked to environmental toxins, although causation is difficult to prove. One expert who has extensively studied the breast cancer/environment connection is Megan Schwarzman, a research scientist at the University of California–Berkeley's School of Public Health. "We wouldn't want to suggest that the environment is the most important cause or is the only cause of breast cancer," says Schwarzman. "But it's a very understudied cause and it's also the one that points toward prevention."[31]

Environmental factors have long been suspected as a reason why women in the military have such a high incidence of breast cancer compared with women in the civilian population. "It is a well-documented fact," says retired US Army lieutenant colonel Leonard L. Boswell, "that one of the highest forms of cancer among our service members and veterans is breast cancer."[32] A study that focused on this fact was conducted in 2009 by physicians from Walter Reed Army Medical Center. The team examined the incidence of several types of cancer, including breast cancer, and compared it with cancer among military personnel and people in the general population. The study analyzed data from the US Department of Defense's Automated Central Tumor Registry, as well as from nine NCI registries.

> " When scientists investigate environmental causes of breast cancer, one of their main focuses is chemicals. "

At the conclusion of the study, the team confirmed that incidence rates of certain types of cancer were significantly higher among military personnel. Breast cancer, for instance, was found to affect military women at rates up to 40 percent higher than the general population—with more women affected by the disease between 2000 and 2011 than were wounded in Iraq and Afghanistan. Although it is not entirely clear why the prevalence is so high among women in the military, theories include the high use of birth control pills (a known risk factor for breast cancer), as well as job exposure to electromagnetic radiation and volatile chemicals.

One woman who developed breast cancer after spending four years in the US Air Force was Jennifer Matarazzo. One year after leaving the military, she was diagnosed at the age of twenty-six. "My diagnosis . . . came as a complete shock," says Matarazzo. She has no history of cancer in her family, and she has always been healthy and in good physical condition. "Obviously I can't pinpoint what caused my cancer, but I've always wondered if it was in any way connected to various exposures during my service. I can't help but be a bit suspicious."[33]

Chemical Culprits

When scientists investigate environmental causes of breast cancer, one of their main focuses is chemicals. This sort of research is challenging for a number of reasons, such as the sheer volume of chemicals that exist and the fact that breast cancer is a complex disease. The Breast Cancer Fund writes: "The time between exposures and development of the disease may be decades; we may not know what chemicals we've been exposed to; and we are not exposed to chemicals in isolation."[34]

The link between chemicals and breast cancer was one focus of the 2009 Walter Reed study. Military women typically perform heavy industrial jobs such as working as auto mechanics and motor transport operators. Thus, they have a high likelihood of being exposed to toxic chemicals that may contribute to the development of breast cancer. In the published report, which appeared in the June 2009 issue of the medical journal *Cancer Epidemiology, Biomarkers & Prevention*, the authors write: "Military women are . . . more likely to be engaged in industrial jobs than females in the general population and hence potentially more likely to be exposed to chemicals that may be related to breast cancer."[35]

> "People who are found to have an abnormal breast cancer gene are usually those with a strong family history of breast cancer and/or ovarian cancer."

In its report the team cites a prior study that was conducted by researchers from the Navy Environmental Health Center in Portsmouth, Virginia, and published in September 2005. Age-adjusted breast cancer incidence rates were calculated for 270,000 enlisted women who served in the US Army from 1980 to 1996. The team concluded that for enlisted women under age thirty-five who worked regularly with at least one volatile organic compound (such as solvents, paints, and exhaust) were 48 percent more likely to develop breast cancer than those who were not exposed to the chemicals. This level of risk was confirmed by the Walter Reed researchers in 2009.

Workers at Risk

Women in the private sector who are exposed to chemicals are also at risk of developing breast cancer. This was the focus of a six-year study, published in November 2012, that was conducted by a team of researchers from Canada, the United States, and the United Kingdom. The research project was prompted by suspicions that women working in automotive parts factories in the Canadian city of Windsor, Ontario, were suffering from unusually high rates of breast cancer. In the course of performing their jobs, these workers regularly handled a wide array of chemicals, solvents, heavy metals, and flame retardants. Many of these substances are known carcinogens, meaning they have been associated with cancer.

> **When scientists talk about potential causes of breast cancer, obesity is often mentioned as a risk factor, especially in women who have gone through menopause.**

The research team investigated the occupational histories of 2,152 women from Ontario's Essex and Kent Counties: 1,006 women who had breast cancer and 1,146 who did not. To ensure accurate comparisons, the team made adjustments for smoking, weight, alcohol use, and other lifestyle and reproductive factors. By the end of the study, the team had found that women who worked in the automotive plastics industry were nearly five times as likely to develop breast cancer prior to menopause as those who did not work in that industry. When the findings were released, Breast Cancer Fund president Jeanne Rizzo called it a "very powerful piece of work." She welcomed the research team's efforts, saying that "the piece that's really been missing for female breast cancer is occupation."[36]

A Family Matter

Although a number of genes have been associated with hereditary breast cancer, most cases result from mutations in the BRCA1 or BRCA2 genes. People who carry one or both of these abnormalities have a substantially higher lifetime risk of developing breast cancer than those without the genetic mutation. According to the Pink Lotus Breast Center, women carrying BRCA1 or BRCA2 gene mutations have as much as an 87 percent lifetime risk of breast cancer, compared with 12 percent among women in the general population.

People who are found to have an abnormal breast cancer gene are usually those with a strong family history of breast cancer and/or ovarian cancer. Their risk is also higher if gland-related cancers (pancreatic, colon, thyroid) run in the family, and if one or more male relatives have had breast cancer. But, says Breastcancer.org, "If one family member has an abnormal breast cancer gene, it does not mean that all family members will have it."[37]

Vulnerable Populations

Research has consistently shown that certain groups have a higher-than-normal likelihood of carrying mutated BRCA1 and/or BRCA2 genes. One example of such a group is Ashkenazi Jews. According to the CDC, about one out of every forty Ashkenazi Jews has this genetic mutation, compared with one out of eight hundred people in the general population. This applies not only to women but also to men, as the Fred Hutchinson Cancer Research Center writes: "Just as Ashkenazi women have an increased risk of inheriting a mutated BRCA1 and BRCA2 gene from one or both of their parents, so do Ashkenazi men. These mutations result in a higher risk of developing certain types of cancer, including male breast cancer and prostate cancer."[38]

African American women also have an especially high prevalence of BRCA mutations. This was one finding of a study released in June 2013 by University of Chicago oncologist Jane Churpek and her colleagues. The team investigated 249 African American breast cancer patients who received genetic counseling from 1992 to 2011. Compared with the general population, in which 5 to 10 percent of women with breast cancer have genetic mutations, 22 percent of the black women in

> **Although scientists have learned a great deal about breast cancer over the years, they are the first to acknowledge that the exact cause remains unknown.**

Churpek's study had what she calls "a clearly damaging mutation."[39] Of the abnormal genes identified in the study, 79 percent were BRCA1 or BRCA2, and 21 percent were other genes with known cancer risk.

Another 2013 study focused on Japanese women with breast cancer and revealed that they also have an unusually high prevalence of BRCA gene mutations. A team of researchers from the Japanese Breast Cancer Society conducted genetic testing on 260 Japanese women whose female family members had breast cancer. They found that one-third of the women carried mutations in BRCA1 or BRCA2 genes, with one of the women having mutations in both genes. A June 2013 article about the study explains: "Particularly alarming, the study found women with a mutation in their BRCA1 genes are four times more likely to develop a type of breast cancer that is not responsive to hormones or anticancer drugs."[40]

Obesity Ups the Risk

When scientists talk about potential causes of breast cancer, obesity is often mentioned as a risk factor, especially in women who have gone through menopause. In an April 2012 report, Seattle, Washington, researchers Garnet L. Anderson and Marian L. Neuhouser write: "Obesity has been consistently associated with an increased risk of postmenopausal breast cancer in population-based studies."[41] One reason for this connection is that fat cells produce excess amounts of hormones such as estrogen and insulin, which fuel the growth of cancerous tumors. Also, fat increases inflammation, which is another factor in cancer development.

Obesity has also been found to increase a person's risk of having breast cancer come back after a period of remission. In 2012 New York oncologist Joseph A. Sparano and his colleagues released a study that involved evaluation of data from more than seven thousand female breast cancer patients. Among women with hormone-sensitive tumors, those who were overweight or obese when they were diagnosed were about 30 percent more likely to have a recurrence of breast cancer after being treated with surgery and chemotherapy than those with normal body weight. What this means, according to University of Miami oncologist Stefan Gluck, is that "the more you weigh, the worse the outcome."[42]

Another study that examined the connection between obesity and breast cancer was published in 2011 by researchers at the Fred Hutchinson Cancer Research Center. The team analyzed data from 155,723 women enrolled in the Women's Health Initiative, a program of the National Institutes of Health. They assessed body mass index (a measure of weight in proportion to height) and recreational physical activity among 2,917 women who were diagnosed with breast cancer, including 307 with triple-negative breast cancer and 2,610 with estrogen receptor–

positive breast cancer (in which the cancer is fed by estrogen). The team found that women with the highest body mass index had a 35 percent increased risk of triple-negative breast cancers and a 39 percent increased risk of estrogen receptor–positive breast cancers. In contrast, the women who reported high rates of physical activity had a 23 percent decreased risk of triple-negative breast cancer and a 15 percent decreased risk of estrogen receptor–positive breast cancer. Thus, obesity and lack of physical activity heightened the breast cancer risk, whereas an active lifestyle had the opposite effect.

Complex Causes

Although scientists have learned a great deal about breast cancer over the years, they are the first to acknowledge that the exact cause remains unknown. Genetic mutations are definitely a contributing factor, but they are only part of the story, along with environmental toxins and other potential risk factors. As research continues, more answers will undoubtedly be found. Los Angeles surgeon Susan Love, author of *Dr. Susan Love's Breast Book*, shares her thoughts: "With all the money that we've put into breast cancer, we're still asking the same questions: What causes it? We need to start getting a little more creative."[43]

What Causes Breast Cancer?

Most breast cancer isn't inherited, but when it is, it's devastating.

—Mary-Claire King, interviewed by Sara Reardon, "Court Ruling on Genes Is a 'Victory for Common Sense,'" *New Scientist*, June 18, 2013. www.newscientist.com.

King, who is a professor at the University of Washington–Seattle, is a geneticist who discovered the BRCA1 gene in 1990.

The biggest single risk factor for breast cancer is age, a risk that is always increasing.

—Carey K. Anders and Nancy U. Lin, *100 Questions and Answers About Triple Negative Breast Cancer*. Burlington, MA: Jones & Bartlett, 2012.

Anders is a clinician-scientist and an assistant professor of medicine at the University of North Carolina, and Lin is a medical oncologist in the Department of Medical Oncology at the Dana-Farber Cancer Institute.

* Editor's Note: While the definition of a primary source can be narrowly or broadly defined, for the purposes of Compact Research, a primary source consists of: 1) results of original research presented by an organization or researcher; 2) eyewitness accounts of events, personal experience, or work experience; 3) first-person editorials offering pundits' opinions; 4) government officials presenting political plans and/or policies; 5) representatives of organizations presenting testimony or policy.

❝Researchers have identified some inherited gene mutations that are known to contribute to the development of certain types of cancer.❞

—Cancer Treatment Centers of America, "Breast Cancer Risk Factors," 2013. ww2.cancercenter.com.

Cancer Treatment Centers of America is a national network of hospitals focusing on complex and advanced-stage cancer.

❝Having a first-degree relative (mother, sister, daughter) with breast cancer poses the greatest risk to other female members of the family—three to five times that of the general population.❞

—Cleveland Clinic Breast Center, *Breast Cancer Treatment Guide*, 2012. http://my.clevelandclinic.org.

The Cleveland Clinic Breast Center provides patient care for the screening, diagnosis, and treatment of all medical and cosmetic breast problems.

❝News stories exploring the links between breast cancer and the environment are popping up all over the place.❞

—Breast Cancer Fund, "Breast Cancer Ties to Environment Probed (*San Francisco Chronicle*, 2/27/13)," *Inside Prevention* (blog), February 28, 2013. www.insideprevention.org.

The Breast Cancer Fund identifies and advocates for elimination of environmental and other preventable causes of breast cancer.

❝Alcohol also puts you at risk: As little as three glasses per week increases your risk of breast cancer.❞

—Powel H. Brown, interviewed by Marc Silver, "Angelina Jolie's News: Docs Talk About Breast Cancer," *National Geographic*, May 15, 2013. http://news.nationalgeographic.com.

Brown is a breast medical oncologist and professor/chair of the Department of Clinical Cancer Prevention at the University of Texas MD Anderson Cancer Center.

❝Many women who develop breast cancer have no known risk factors other than simply being women.❞

—Mayo Clinic, "Breast Cancer," May 22, 2013. www.mayoclinic.com.

—The Mayo Clinic is a world-renowned health-care facility that is dedicated to patient care, education, and research.

❝Taking oral contraceptives ('the pill') may slightly increase the risk of breast cancer in current users. This risk decreases over time.❞

—National Cancer Institute, "Breast Cancer Prevention (PDQ)," May 31, 2013. www.cancer.gov.

The NCI is the federal government's principal agency for cancer research and training.

❝Hormones seem to play a role in many cases of breast cancer, but just how this happens is not fully understood.❞

—American Cancer Society, "Do We Know What Causes Breast Cancer?," February 26, 2013. www.cancer.org.

The American Cancer Society is a nationwide, community-based volunteer health organization that is dedicated to eliminating cancer as a major health problem.

Facts and Illustrations

What Causes Breast Cancer?

- According to the CDC, only about **47 percent** of breast cancer cases in the United States can be attributed to established risk factors.

- The American Cancer Society states that women who have a **first-degree relative** (mother, sister, or daughter) with a history of breast cancer are about twice as likely to develop breast cancer as women who do not have this family history.

- According to the group Living Beyond Breast Cancer, being premenopausal, African American, Hispanic, or of Caribbean descent increases someone's chances of developing **triple-negative breast cancer**.

- The Memorial Sloan-Kettering Cancer Center states that about **one in five men** who develop breast cancer have a mother, sister, or daughter with the disease.

- According to Breastcancer.org, about **90 percent** of breast cancers are due to genetic abnormalities that happen as a result of the aging process and the "wear and tear" of life in general.

- Cancer Treatment Centers of America states that **race** is a factor in who develops inflammatory breast cancer, with African American women at greater risk than white women.

- According to the Triple Negative Breast Cancer Foundation, if people who have the **BRCA1** mutation develop breast cancer before age fifty, it is often found to be triple-negative breast cancer.

Out-of-Control Cell Growth

Although much remains unknown about breast cancer, including its cause, scientists do know that it begins with uncontrolled cell growth. Under normal circumstances, when cells grow old or become damaged they die and are replaced by new cells, which is known as apoptosis. But sometimes the process goes wrong, and genetic material of a cell becomes damaged or changed, producing mutations. Thus, rather than dying as they should, mutated cells begin growing out of control to form new, abnormal cells that can lead to development of a mass of tissue, or tumor.

Normal Versus Cancerous Cells

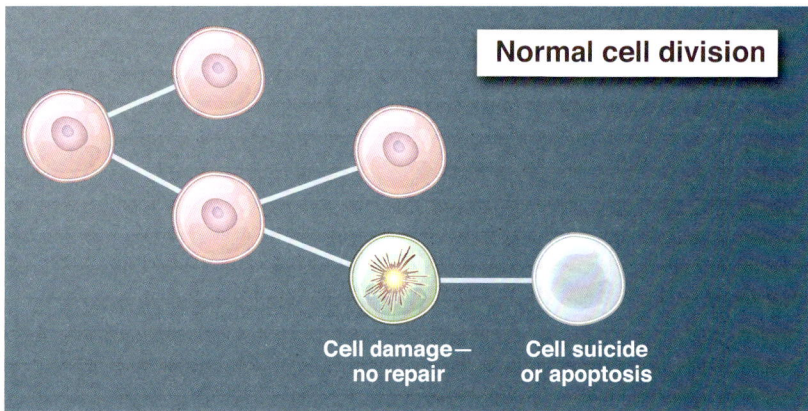

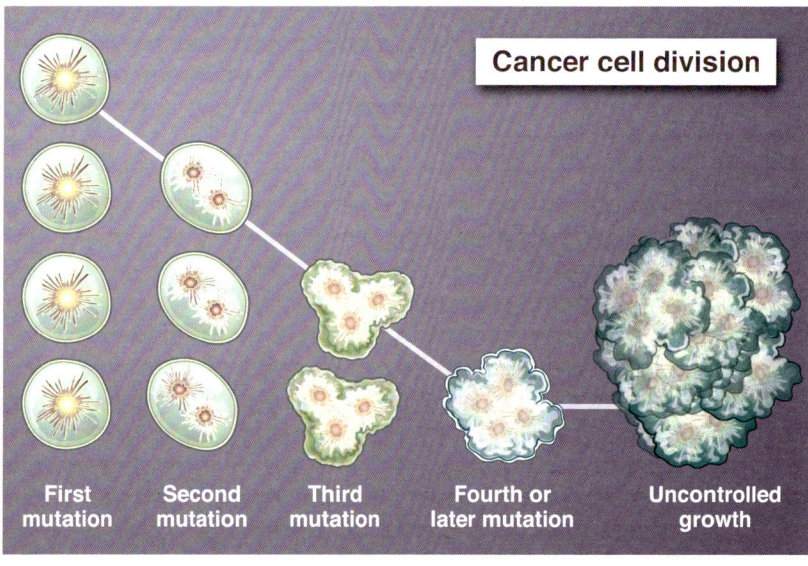

Normal cell division

Cell damage—
no repair

Cell suicide
or apoptosis

Cancer cell division

| First mutation | Second mutation | Third mutation | Fourth or later mutation | Uncontrolled growth |

Source: National Cancer Institute, "What Is Cancer?," February 8, 2013. www.cancer.gov.

A Complex Collection of Risk Factors

Scientists do not know the exact cause of breast cancer, but they have identified a number of factors that can increase the risk of developing it. As shown here, some of these risk factors are unavoidable, whereas others are lifestyle choices.

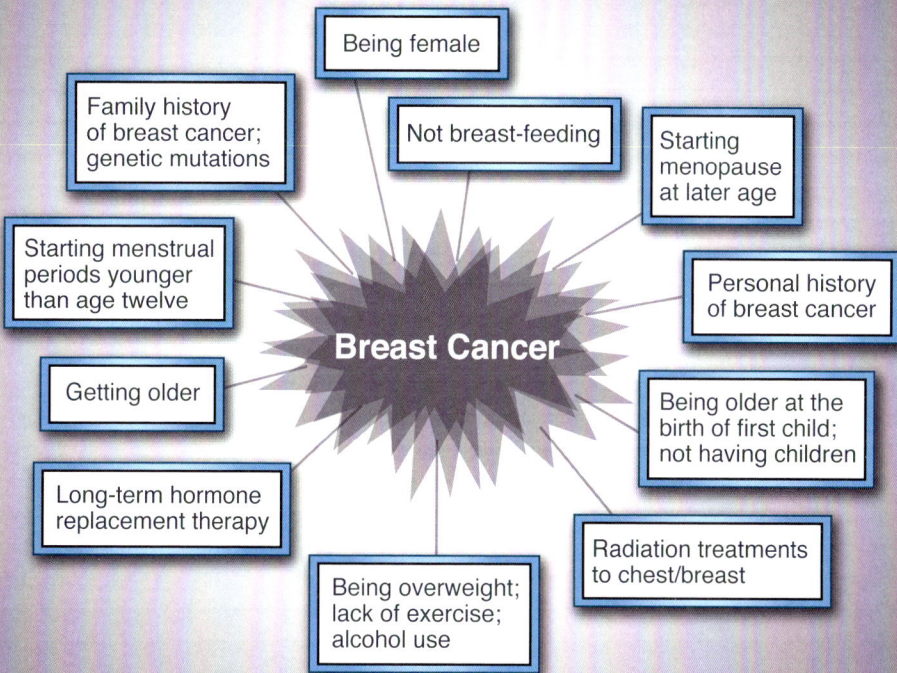

Being female

Family history of breast cancer; genetic mutations

Not breast-feeding

Starting menopause at later age

Starting menstrual periods younger than age twelve

Breast Cancer

Personal history of breast cancer

Getting older

Being older at the birth of first child; not having children

Long-term hormone replacement therapy

Radiation treatments to chest/breast

Being overweight; lack of exercise; alcohol use

Source: Centers for Disease Control and Prevention, "Risk Factors," May 8, 2013. www.cdc.gov.

- According to the NCI, unlike cancer of the lungs and several other types of cancer, it has not been proved that either active **cigarette smoking** or **inhaling secondhand smoke** increases the risk of developing breast cancer.

- The National Breast Cancer Foundation states that there is an increased risk of breast cancer for women who have used **birth control pills** for more than five years.

Genetic Mutation Increases Risk

Cancer experts estimate that 5 to 10 percent of breast cancer cases are caused by a hereditary genetic mutation, meaning that a damaged gene was inherited from a parent. The most common genetic mutations known to scientists are BRCA1 or BRCA2, and women who carry one of these mutations have a much higher risk for developing breast cancer than those who do not. As shown here, the risk increases substantially as people get older.

Lifetime risk of developing breast cancer by decade of life:

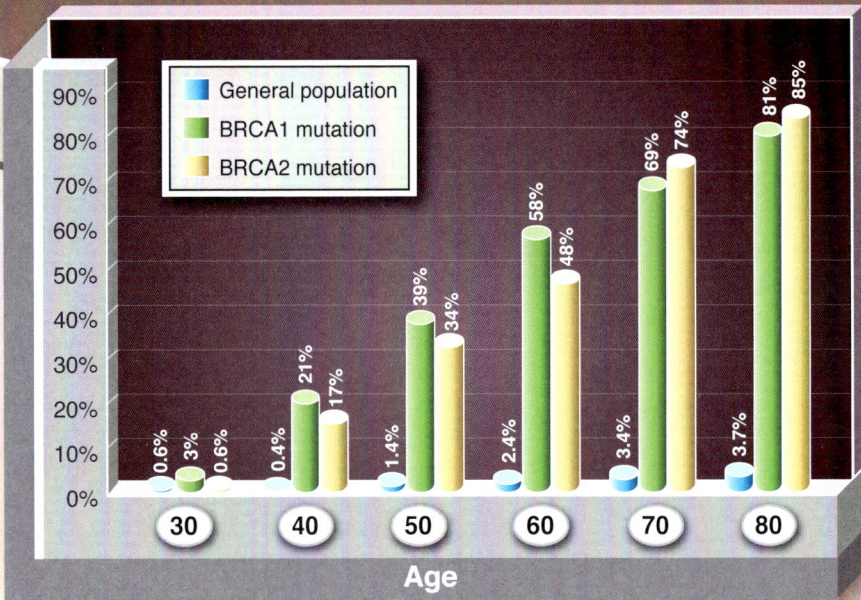

Legend:
- General population
- BRCA1 mutation
- BRCA2 mutation

Age	General population	BRCA1 mutation	BRCA2 mutation
30	0.6%	3%	0.6%
40	0.4%	21%	17%
50	1.4%	39%	34%
60	2.4%	58%	48%
70	3.4%	69%	74%
80	3.7%	81%	85%

Source: Pink Lotus Breast Center, "Breast Cancer 101," May 14, 2013. http://pinklotusbreastcenter.com.

- According to the Memorial Sloan-Kettering Cancer Center, age is a strong factor in who develops breast cancer: **80 percent** of cases develop in women over age fifty.

- Breastcancer.org states that men who have an abnormal **BRCA1** gene have a risk of developing breast cancer that is about **80 times greater** than average.

How Successful Are Breast Cancer Treatments?

66Breast cancer is not a death sentence. Caught early on, tumors can be removed and many women live long and healthy lives cancer free after receiving the diagnosis.99

—Kathleen Ruddy, an internationally recognized breast cancer surgeon who is founder and president of the Breast Health & Healing Foundation.

66The past few decades have seen huge advances in treatment, but about one-quarter of those diagnosed will die from the disease. Complicating matters, breast cancers are remarkably diverse, and tumour cells seem to hide in 'cured' individuals.99

—Michelle Grayson, senior editor for the publication *Nature Outlook.*

If ever someone could be considered a success story for breast cancer treatment, it is Heather Young. She was thirty-one years old and had just given birth to her second child when she noticed obvious changes in her breast. "I felt a really large lump overnight basically," she says. "My breast was red, hot and swollen and it just kept growing, getting really painful." After a series of outpatient tests that stretched over several weeks, Young was admitted to the hospital for further testing. She learned that she had inflammatory breast cancer—and that her prognosis was dismal. "The doctor came in at about 11 o'clock at night," she says, "and told me I had end-stage breast cancer and that maybe I only had a couple of months to live."[44] Young was devastated but she vowed to do everything possible to fight the cancer.

Her treatment program was multifaceted and aggressive. She underwent a mastectomy, which was followed by six months of chemotherapy. She also went through seven weeks of radiation treatment and had five breast reconstruction surgeries. As of October 2012 the woman who was told she had only a couple of months to live had been cancer-free for eight years. Young's personal experience with the disease and her triumph over it motivated her to change careers and become an oncology nurse. That enables her to give hope, comfort, and inspiration to other patients who are waging their own difficult battles against cancer.

One Day at a Time

Young's treatment program was customized for her individual needs, which is typical for breast cancer patients. Most people who are diagnosed with the disease undergo surgery to remove cancerous tissue. This may be a lumpectomy; a partial mastectomy; or a complete mastectomy, which often involves removal of some lymph nodes if the cancer has started to spread.

Typically, surgery is accompanied by companion treatments that are known as adjuvant therapies. The NCI explains:

> Even in early-stage breast cancer, cells may break away from the primary tumor and spread to other parts of the body (metastasize). Therefore, doctors give adjuvant therapy to kill any cancer cells that may have spread, even if they cannot be detected by imaging or laboratory tests. Studies have shown that adjuvant therapy for breast cancer may increase the chance of long-term survival by preventing a recurrence.[45]

Typical adjuvant therapies include chemotherapy, radiation treatment, and targeted therapy, which uses drugs to attack cancer cells while doing little or no damage to normal cells.

Paula Mitchell Joseph was successfully treated for breast cancer in 2005 when she was in her early fifties—but when she was first diagnosed, all she could think about was dying. "I just sat there, staring at the surgeon," she says, "and felt the blood drain out of my head. I asked him, 'Is this a death sentence?' and he said it wasn't. But what got to me was his attitude. He was so nonchalant as he sat there making no eye contact with me, flipping through papers in my folder like nothing was out of the ordinary. In the meantime, I'm thinking, 'My God, what am I going to do? I'm dying!' It was the worst day of my life."[46]

Once Joseph recovered from the initial shock, she was motivated to get started with treatment right away—but with a different surgeon. Initially, she wanted to have her entire breast removed, thinking that would be the best way to keep the cancer from coming back. But her new doctor assured her that with the type of cancer she had, a lumpectomy would be just as effective. So in August 2005 she had the operation, followed by several months of chemotherapy and radiation treatments. For the next six years, she took medications that stopped her ovaries from producing estrogen.

> " Typical adjuvant therapies include chemotherapy, radiation treatment, and targeted therapy, which uses drugs to attack cancer cells while doing little or no damage to normal cells. "

Joseph has remained cancer-free since she her last treatment in 2007. She does not allow herself to dwell on negative thoughts, but she admits that a little bit of fear is always tucked away in the back of her mind. "You always have the fear," she says. "I know that as more time passes my chances of having a recurrence get slimmer and slimmer . . . but the reality is, with cancer there's no such thing as 'five years and you're home free.' So I just take each day at a time, focus on what's really important, and try to get as much out of life as I possibly can."[47]

Triple-Negative Treatment

Cancer specialists widely agree that triple-negative breast cancer is one of the most challenging types to treat. Linda Vahdat, who directs the Breast Cancer Research Program at Weill Cornell Medical College in

New York City, says that triple-negative breast cancer "tends to grow very differently than 'regular' breast cancer, and we don't have the same tools to treat it. There are far fewer options, and there's no triple-negative directed therapy, so far."[48] Unlike more common types of breast cancer, triple-negative is not fueled by the hormones estrogen and progesterone or by the human epidermal growth factor receptor 2 (HER2). Thus, it does not respond to medications that are designed for those types.

This does not mean, however, that triple-negative breast cancer is untreatable, as it can be successfully treated if caught early enough. "Chemotherapy is an effective treatment," says Breastcancer.org. "Research shows that triple negative breast cancer may even respond better to chemotherapy than other types of breast cancer. Surgery and radiation therapy are also usually used."[49] Still, options are limited for people diagnosed with triple-negative breast cancer, and their disease is challenging to treat. For that reason, scientists are aggressively pursuing research in an effort to find new and better ways of treating it.

> " **Cancer specialists widely agree that triple-negative breast cancer is one of the most challenging types to treat.** "

In experimental trials a drug that has shown remarkable promise in preventing breast cancer relapse is tetrathiomolybdate, better known as TM. Designed to remove copper from the body, TM is typically used to treat patients with a rare genetic disorder called Wilson's disease, which causes a buildup of excess copper in the body. TM works by binding with excess copper in the bloodstream; the copper is then excreted in waste material. This treatment is important for breast cancer patients because copper is essential for the metastatic process. By removing copper from their bodies, says Vahdat, the drug could be "keeping tumors that want to spread in a dormant state."[50]

In a small study led by Vahdat, 81 percent of the patients with metastatic triple-negative breast cancer who took TM were relapse-free after ten months. One of the women with an extremely aggressive and advanced form of the cancer began taking the experimental drug in 2007 and was still free of cancer six years later. Although the researchers do not know if TM will be an effective mainstream treatment for breast cancer, they are optimistic about its potential. Vahdat, who refers to the study as a "very exciting and promising result," says that more research on the drug is necessary, but breast cancer patients are already excited about it. "There's a lot of interest in this," she says. "We'll see. We're all scientists and we want to make sure that what we say we're doing is true."[51]

Trying to See the Bright Side

One chemotherapy drug that is often given to women with breast cancer is Adriamycin, a bright red liquid that is delivered intravenously. Patients have been known to refer to the drug as the "red devil" because of its horribly unpleasant side effects: hair loss, severe nausea, constipation, and sores in the mouth that are so painful it hurts to eat or even talk. "I know what it's like to get the 'red devil' in the veins," says Elaine Schattner, a New York City oncologist who was treated for breast cancer. "It's not an easy drug; my patients knew this and so did I."[52]

Another physician who was treated with Adriamycin for breast cancer is Kimberly Allison of Seattle, Washington. By the time her cancer was diagnosed it was already at stage III and was very aggressive. "I checked on the survival statistics for my kind of cancer," says Allison, "and they were only 40 percent. . . . It seemed like the world had turned on its end."[53] Her tumor was large, so she underwent chemotherapy first, before surgery, to reduce its size. That was when she began taking Adriamycin as part of her presurgery treatment, and she was fiercely determined to endure her experience with a positive attitude. So she renamed the drug "red sunshine" and forced herself to look forward to being treated with it every week, as she explains: "Thinking of that drug as 'red sunshine' helped me see the positive side of a trying situation."[54]

> " One chemotherapy drug that is often given to women with breast cancer is Adriamycin, a bright red liquid that is delivered intravenously. "

By the time Allison was finished with chemotherapy, tests showed that there was no trace of cancer in her bloodstream. Still, she made the decision to have both breasts removed and reconstructed. "I didn't want to go through increased screening my entire life," she says, "which hopefully will be long. And I was mad at my breasts. I felt they had betrayed me, and I wasn't that attached to them."[55] After her mastectomy, the final phase of Allison's treatment was undergoing radiation to kill any errant cancer cells.

Allison's treatment lasted for about a year. Since then she has remained cancer-free, and she wrote a book about her experience called (aptly) *Red Sunshine*. She wanted to reach out to women with breast cancer, especially those who were newly diagnosed, so they could "hear somebody's voice telling them, . . . look, I've been through something similar, and I made it through, and it actually was an enlightening experience in these ways and, you know, to keep a positive attitude about it." Allison has another important goal for her book as well. "My hope," she says, "is that it increases awareness and healing."[56]

> " In 2013 a team of military researchers completed a ten-year study of a vaccine known as E75, which shows enormous potential to protect women against the recurrence of breast cancer. "

A Breast Cancer Vaccine

Many scientists have explored the possibility of developing a vaccination for breast cancer, much the same as vaccines protect people against measles, smallpox, polio, and influenza. In 2013 a team of military researchers completed a ten-year study of a vaccine known as E75, which shows enormous potential to protect women against the recurrence of breast cancer. The vaccine was tested on more than one hundred female soldiers who were recovering from breast cancer, along with a comparable number of civilian women. Physician and US Army colonel George Peoples, who founded the research network Cancer Vaccine Development, says that trial indicated that the vaccine cuts a woman's risk of breast cancer recurring by half. According to Peoples, vaccines can stop the spread of cancers in the same way that they fight infectious diseases—by training the body's immune system to attack cancer cells.

The army's breast cancer vaccine trial was conducted at numerous military medical facilities as well as at twelve civilian facilities. All the women who participated were recovering from breast cancer surgery, chemotherapy, and/or radiation therapy. The women were all vaccinated and then followed by the research team for several years to gauge whether the vaccine could slow the recurrence rate. The findings were promising, as Peoples explains: "We found that the patients who were vaccinated had a recurrence rate that was half of non-vaccinated women."[57]

One woman who participated in the trial is fifty-two-year-old Raquel Gutierrez, whose husband is an air force retiree. Gutierrez was diagnosed with breast cancer in January 2010 and underwent surgery to have a lump removed, followed by months of chemotherapy and radiation therapy. She joined Peoples's vaccine study in October 2011 and had a series of vaccine injections at San Antonio Military Medical Center and Lackland Air Force Base. She hopes that the vaccine will keep the disease from coming back, as she explains: "Having the vaccine has given me the feeling that I've got a better chance of recovery."[58]

Hope for the Future

Just hearing the words "you have breast cancer" is enough to strike terror in anyone's heart. Yet those who are diagnosed with the disease can take comfort in the fact that because of improved treatments, many breast cancer patients today are living longer than ever before. Another positive aspect is that breast cancer research is considered a high priority, which means that even more treatment options will likely be developed in the coming years. Perhaps sometime in the not-so-distant future, scientists will announce that they have found a cure—and that day cannot possibly come soon enough for anyone who is battling this dreaded disease.

How Successful Are Breast Cancer Treatments?

"Although breast cancer is a very frightening and dangerous disease, most women diagnosed with breast cancer are cured completely."

—Carey K. Anders and Nancy U. Lin, *100 Questions and Answers About Triple Negative Breast Cancer.* Burlington, MA: Jones & Bartlett, 2012.

Anders is a clinician-scientist and an assistant professor of medicine at the University of North Carolina, and Lin is a medical oncologist in the Department of Medical Oncology at the Dana-Farber Cancer Institute.

"We still do not know how to cure breast cancer."

—National Breast Cancer Coalition, "Myth #20: With New Treatments, We Can Now Cure Breast Cancer," 2013. www.breastcancerdeadline2020.org.

The National Breast Cancer Coalition is a grassroots advocacy organization that is committed to improving public policies for breast cancer research, diagnosis, and treatment.

"While systemic chemotherapy and hormonal therapy play vital roles in the management of breast cancer, radiation therapy (RT) too plays a critical role in improvement in both local control and survival."

—Alphonse G. Taghian and Michele Y. Halyard, eds., *Breast Cancer*. New York: Demos Medical, 2012.

Taghian is chief of breast radiation oncology at Massachusetts General Hospital, and Halyard is a radiation oncologist with the Mayo Clinic in Scottsdale, Arizona.

....

"The increase in breast cancer survival seen since the mid-1970s has been attributed to both screening and improved treatment."

—National Cancer Institute, "Cancer Advances in Focus," September 23, 2010. www.cancer.gov.

The NCI is the federal government's principal agency for cancer research and training.

....

"A man's chance of surviving breast cancer is similar to that of a woman diagnosed at the same stage of disease. Male breast cancer is more likely to be cured if it is discovered early."

—Memorial Sloan-Kettering Cancer Center, "Breast Cancer, Male: About Male Breast Cancer," 2013. www.mskcc.org.

The Memorial Sloan-Kettering Cancer Center is the world's oldest and largest private cancer center and is ranked by *U.S. News & World Report* as one of the top facilities of its kind in the United States.

....

"No alternative medicine treatments have been found to cure breast cancer."

—Mayo Clinic, "Breast Cancer," May 22, 2013. www.mayoclinic.com.

—The Mayo Clinic is a world-renowned health-care facility that is dedicated to patient care, education, and research.

....

“Some people may think that their chemotherapy treatment is not working if they do not experience side effects. However, this is a myth. Side effects differ from one patient to another.”

—Cleveland Clinic Breast Center, *Breast Cancer Treatment Guide*, 2012. http://my.clevelandclinic.org.

The Cleveland Clinic Breast Center provides patient care for the screening, diagnosis, and treatment of all medical and cosmetic breast problems.

“Some patients are given treatment, such as chemotherapy or hormone therapy, before surgery. The goal of this treatment is to shrink the tumor in the hope it will allow a less extensive operation to be done.”

—American Cancer Society, “How Is Breast Cancer Treated?,” February 26, 2013. www.cancer.org.

The American Cancer Society is a nationwide, community-based volunteer health organization that is dedicated to eliminating cancer as a major health problem.

How Successful Are Breast Cancer Treatments?

- According to the Cleveland Clinic Breast Center, the death rate from breast cancer has dropped about **2 percent** per year since 1990 as a result of better awareness and improved treatment options, along with earlier diagnosis.

- The NCI states that the breast cancer death rate has been **declining** since 1989, when it peaked at a rate of thirty-three deaths for every one hundred thousand women.

- According to Susan G. Komen for a Cure, there are more than **2.9 million** breast cancer survivors in the United States, which represents the largest group of cancer survivors in the country.

- The Dr. Susan Love Research Foundation states that most invasive breast cancers have been present for eight to ten years by the time they are detected on a **mammogram or by a physical exam**.

- According to the Metastatic Breast Cancer Network, **metastatic breast cancer** can occur five, ten, or fifteen years after a person's original diagnosis.

- Johns Hopkins Medicine states that the majority of individuals diagnosed and treated for breast cancer will never experience **recurrence** of the disease.

Chemotherapy After Surgery Improves Survival Rates

A 2012 study by a team of researchers from Switzerland focused on women who had a recurrence of breast cancer that had not spread beyond nearby tissue. The team found that patients who underwent chemotherapy after surgery had better survival rates.

Rate of cancer-free and overall survival, with and without chemotherapy

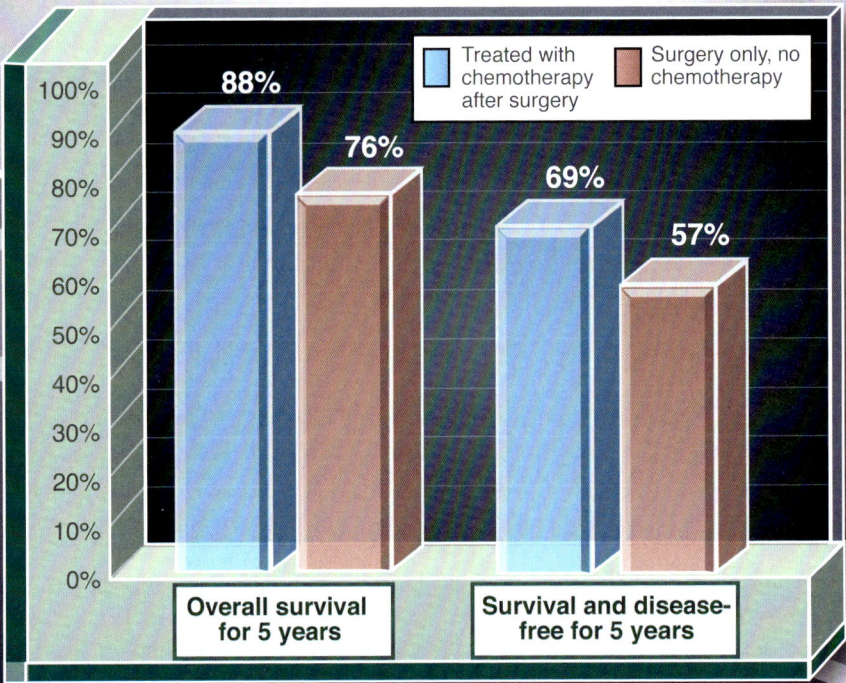

Treated with chemotherapy after surgery

Surgery only, no chemotherapy

88%

76%

69%

57%

Overall survival for 5 years

Survival and disease-free for 5 years

Source: National Cancer Institute, "Chemotherapy After Surgery Improves Survival When Some Breast Cancers Return," *NCI Cancer Bulletin*, December 11, 2012.

- In a 2013 study of Japanese women whose female family members had breast cancer, researchers found that women with a mutation in their BRCA1 genes were four times more likely to develop a type of breast cancer that is not responsive to **hormones or anticancer drugs**.

Steadily Improving Survival Rates

According to the American Cancer Society, the five-year relative survival rate for women with breast cancer has increased since 1975 from 75 percent to 90 percent. The group attributes this progress to a combination of early detection and improvements in breast cancer treatment.

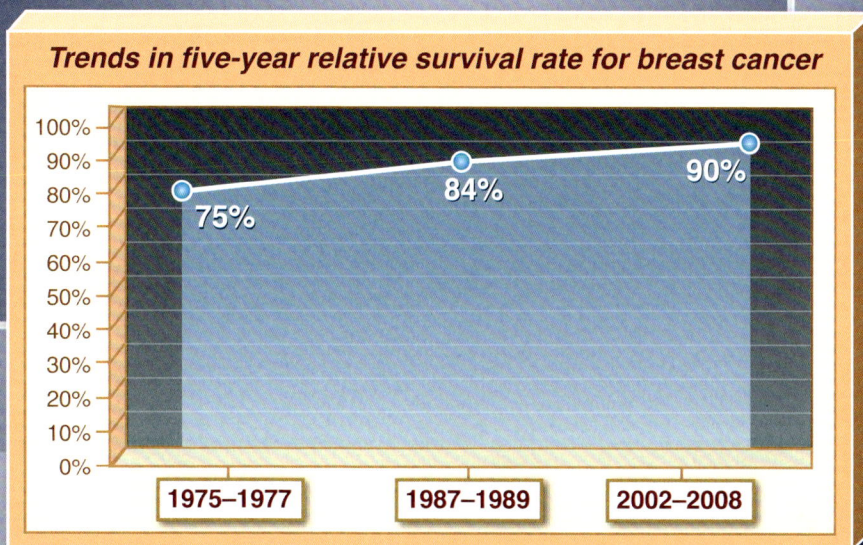

Trends in five-year relative survival rate for breast cancer

75%

84%

90%

| 1975–1977 | 1987–1989 | 2002–2008 |

Source: American Cancer Society, "Cancer Facts & Figures 2013," January 17, 2013. www.cancer.org.

- According to the National Breast Cancer Foundation, **ductal carcinoma** in situ is a very early form of breast cancer that is highly treatable; however, if it is left untreated or goes undetected, it can spread into the surrounding breast tissue.

- According to the NCI, **lumpectomy followed by radiation** therapy has replaced mastectomy as the preferred surgical approach for treating early stage breast cancer.

- The Cleveland Clinic Breast Center states that most breast cancer recurrences occur in the first **three to five years** after initial treatment.

Promising Experimental Treatment

A type of breast cancer known as HER2-positive is extremely aggressive and challenging to treat. So in June 2012, breast cancer specialists were enthusiastic to hear about a new experimental treatment that shows great promise. In a clinical trial conducted by a team of Duke University researchers, nearly a thousand patients with HER2-positive breast cancer were divided into two groups: one, whose members were given the experimental drug T-DM1, and the other (control group), whose members took a standard combination-drug treatment. As this graph shows, 65 percent of the T-DM1 participants were still alive after two years compared with 48 percent of the control group. Scientists say that this is a promising finding that could bring new hope to women diagnosed with HER2-positive metastatic breast cancer.

Survival rates among women with HER2-positive metastatic breast cancer two years following onset of treatment

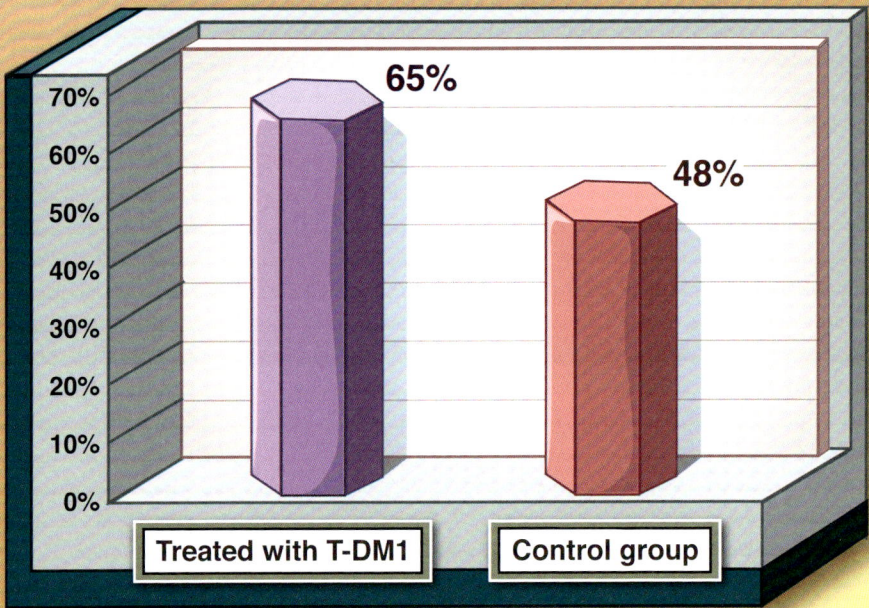

Source: American Society of Clinical Oncology, "Major Advances," *Clinical Cancer Advances 2012*, September 27, 2012. www.cancerprogress.net.

- According to Johns Hopkins Medicine, the survival rates and prognoses for men with breast cancer is not as good as it is for women; males have a **25 percent** higher mortality rate than females.

Can Breast Cancer Be Prevented?

I n February 2013 a federal advisory committee issued a strong message about breast cancer research in the United States: Even though "prevention is the key to reducing the burden of breast cancer," preventing the disease has clearly not been a priority for federal research funding. In its formal report the committee explained that "investments in breast cancer research have focused primarily on diagnosis and cure. Comparatively speaking, there are remarkably few examples of advances in the area of breast cancer prevention."[59]

Established by the US Department of Health and Human Services, the committee is made up of scientists, physicians, government officials, and advocacy groups. Legislation passed in 2008 defined its task as evaluating the state of breast cancer research, pointing out knowledge gaps, and making recommendations for improvements. Committee members worked on the project for more than two years, and the 2013 report titled *Breast Cancer and the Environment: Prioritizing Prevention* was the result of those efforts. After discovering that only about 10 percent of breast cancer research focuses on prevention, the group urged the Department of Health and Human Services to start taking steps to remedy that. "Breast cancer prevention is underfunded at the federal level," the report authors wrote, "in both research and public health programs, and future investments must focus on this area."[60]

Efforts to Reduce Risk

Although prevention is not assured, many breast cancer specialists and advocacy groups emphasize that people who eat a nutritious, low-fat diet, are physically active, avoid alcohol, and take other steps to achieve a healthy lifestyle, can reduce their risk of developing cancer, including cancer of the breast. Lillie Shockney, a University Distinguished Service Assistant Professor of Breast Cancer and administrative director of the Johns Hopkins Breast Center who has survived two bouts with breast cancer, shares her thoughts: "Doctors are only beginning to identify lifestyle choices that can influence our cancer risk. These lifestyle choices include diet, exercise, smoking, alcohol, and many other factors. We have control over how we nourish our bodies. This means that we may be able to reduce our breast cancer risk by making smarter choices."[61]

> " According to a study published in the December 2012 issue of the *Journal of the National Cancer Institute*, a healthy diet can reduce the risk of breast cancer; specifically, a diet rich in carotenoids. "

According to a study published in the December 2012 issue of the *Journal of the National Cancer Institute*, a healthy diet can reduce the risk of breast cancer, specifically, a diet rich in carotenoids. These are nutrients found in red-orange fruits and vegetables such as carrots, cantaloupe, tomatoes, sweet potatoes, mangoes, and butternut squash. The study, which was conducted by a team of researchers from the Brigham and Women's Hospital and Harvard Medical School, found that women with the highest blood levels of carotenoids had a 15 to 20 percent lower risk of developing any type of breast cancer. Especially profound was the finding that women with carotenoid-rich diets were shown to have a 40 to 50 percent lower risk of developing the aggressive estrogen receptor–negative breast cancer. Says Heather Eliassen, lead researcher for the study: "Some carotenoids are precursors to vitamin A, which helps regulate cell growth and death. They're also antioxidants, which help eliminate cancer-promoting free radicals."[62]

> " The unfortunate reality is that even the healthiest lifestyle is no guarantee that someone will not develop breast cancer. "

Yet the unfortunate reality is that even the healthiest lifestyle is no guarantee that someone will not develop breast cancer. According to David Gorski, a surgical oncologist who specializes in breast cancer surgery, breast cancer is not as susceptible to lifestyle and diet as some other cancers. He is not saying that adopting a healthy lifestyle has no effect on a person's risk for developing breast cancer, just that the effect tends to be relatively small. Heather Young is living proof of that. Seemingly the poster child for a healthy lifestyle, her breast cancer was a total shock. "I felt like my body had completely failed me," she says, "because I worked out six days a week, I was a health food freak, I never smoked, never drank excessively. I just felt completely betrayed by my body and I was really angry."[63]

The Mammography Controversy

Prominent organizations such as the American Cancer Society and the NCI emphasize that regular mammograms for women over age forty are essential for catching breast cancer at an early stage when it is highly treatable. This has been the standard recommendation and widely accepted practice since the mid-1980s. According to Sandra Swain, a breast cancer specialist who serves as president of the American Society of Clinical Oncology, deaths have "declined dramatically over the past decade"[64] and early detection through mammography has played an important role in that. Swain points out that in women over age fifty, regular screening has reduced breast cancer deaths by as much as 30 percent, and in women aged forty to fifty, by at least 15 percent. "I would recommend that women receive an annual mammogram,"[65] she says.

Not all physicians share Swain's point of view; in fact, in recent years the wisdom of mammography for breast cancer screening has come under fire. Some studies have found that mammograms result in what is termed "overdiagnosis" of breast cancer. H. Gilbert Welch, professor of medicine at the Dartmouth Institute for Health Policy and Clinical Practice, writes: "For decades women have been told that one of the most important things they can do to protect their health is to have regular mammograms. But over the past few years, it's become increasingly clear that these screenings are not all they're cracked up to be."[66]

> **In recent years the wisdom of mammography for breast cancer screening has come under fire.**

Welch, along with his colleagues, conducted an in-depth analysis of national mammography data. They found that between 1976 and 2008, twice as many cases of early stage breast cancer were caught by mammograms, but around 31 percent of those cases involved slow-growing cancers that would never have caused problems. "There was a lot of overdiagnosis," says Welch. "More than a million women who were told they had early stage cancer—most of whom underwent surgery, chemotherapy or radiation—for a 'cancer' that was never going to make them sick." Although Welch does believe that mammography can be useful for certain groups, he maintains that "population-wide screening" should be stopped completely. He writes: "Screening could be targeted instead to those at the highest risk of dying from breast cancer—women with strong family histories or genetic predispositions to the disease. These are the women who are most likely to benefit and least likely to be overdiagnosed."[67]

Welch's study, which was published in the *New England Journal of Medicine* in November 2012, created a stir in the medical science community. Some experts supported its conclusions, while others criticized them harshly. Swain acknowledges that there is disagreement over how frequently women should have mammograms, and she says studies that help broaden scientific understanding can be valuable. She offers words of caution, however, for those who are trying to decide what to do in light of conflicting studies. "Until we have better tools to identify individuals who are most likely to benefit from screening," says Swain, "mammography remains the best available tool for detecting breast cancer in the general population. Our hope is that these studies do not shake women's confidence in the benefits of mammography."[68]

A Permanent Solution

In May 2013 the topic of genetic testing to evaluate breast cancer risk became national (and international) news. In an article written for the *New York Times*, actress Angelina Jolie announced that she had undergone a preventive double mastectomy despite no sign of cancer in either breast. She made this decision because genetic tests showed that she carried the mutated BRCA1 gene, and doctors informed her that she had an 87 percent chance of developing breast cancer.

Jolie's mother, who died in 2007 of ovarian cancer, had also suffered from breast cancer, and both types of cancer affected other women in her family as well. With a strong family history, combined with the genetic abnormality, Jolie was convinced that having both breasts removed was the right thing to do for herself and her children. "The decision to have a mastectomy was not easy," she writes, "but it is one I am very happy that I made. My chances of developing breast cancer have dropped from 87 percent to under 5 percent. I can tell my children that they don't need to fear they will lose me to breast cancer."[69]

No large, formal studies have been conducted to evaluate how common preventive (prophylactic) mastectomies are, but breast cancer specialists can make estimations based on their own observations. According to Kenneth Offit, chief of clinical genetics at the Memorial Sloan-Kettering Cancer Center in New York City, about 30 percent of women who are found to have BRCA mutations choose preventive mastectomies, with those who have seen family members die young from the disease being most likely to opt for the surgery. Another expert is Todd Tuttle, who is chief of surgical oncology at the University of Minnesota.

Tuttle says that since genetic tests to assess breast cancer risk have become available, there has been a surge in the number of women choosing to have their healthy breasts removed.

This has also been the observation of Deanna Attai, a breast cancer surgeon with the Center for Breast Care in Burbank, California. "It does seem like we're doing more of these surgeries," says Attai. "There's an increased awareness about BRCA mutations and breast cancer in general. I think the combination of that plus reconstructive techniques improving gives women a little bit better of an option if they test positive." When asked whether a prophylactic mastectomy is effective in preventing breast cancer, Attai answers with a definitive yes. "With a prophylactic mastectomy, the risk of breast cancer is reduced to about 1 to 3 percent," she says. "So when you look at someone who has maybe a 60 to 80 percent risk of developing breast cancer based on their gene mutation and you can drop that risk down to 1 to 3 percent, that's pretty significant."[70]

> **Just as Angelina Jolie's announcement put prophylactic mastectomies in the national spotlight, it also heightened awareness of genetic testing.**

There is a caveat, however, and Attai says it is an important one. "Despite all of our improvements in plastic and reconstructive surgery, this is still a big deal," she says. "It's not the same as getting a set of implants. There are possibilities of complications with reconstruction. It's a decision women need to think about carefully. It's a significant risk reduction but it's a big decision."[71]

Genetic Testing Pros and Cons

Just as Angelina Jolie's announcement put prophylactic mastectomies in the national spotlight, it also heightened awareness of genetic testing. Olaf Bodamer, a human genetics expert at Miami Miller School of Medicine, says his laboratory started getting calls by women seeking genetic testing soon after Jolie went public with her news. "I think there was an immediate spike following the story in *The New York Times*,"[72] he says. Maxine Chang-Chin, a cancer risk assessment counselor from Broward

County, Florida, says that the article opened the door to important conversations about genetic testing between patients and their doctors. Both Chang-Chin and Bodamer stress, however, that genetic testing should be used judiciously because it is not for everyone.

Johns Hopkins Medicine agrees, saying that people who seek genetic testing do not always consider the negative aspects involved. Aside from the high cost, which can exceed three thousand dollars, there is the possibility of insurance or employment discrimination. "There are some federal and state laws designed to lower the risk of insurance discrimination," the group writes, "but they only pertain to specific types of insurance."[73] There are other risks involved with genetic testing too, such as the emotional turmoil of a positive test result. "An individual who tests positive," says Johns Hopkins Medicine, "may experience anxiety, guilt, depression or fear. Family members may have similar feelings, which could cause strain between relatives."[74]

Prevention Is the Goal

Few things are guaranteed in life, and the certainty of preventing breast cancer is no exception. People can reduce their risk, however, by maintaining a healthy lifestyle, including eating a diet that is low in fat and high in nutrients such as carotenoids, avoiding alcohol, keeping their weight under control, and being physically active. Genetic testing may be advisable for someone who has a strong family history of breast and/or ovarian cancer, although positive test results can lead to some difficult decisions about what to do next. As research continues and scientists learn more about breast cancer and its diverse causes, prevention may be closer to a reality.

Can Breast Cancer Be Prevented?

> **Having regular mammograms can lower the risk of dying from breast cancer.**

—Centers for Disease Control and Prevention, "Kinds of Screening Tests," October 16, 2012. www.cdc.gov.

The CDC is dedicated to protecting health and promoting quality of life through the prevention and control of disease, injury, and disability.

....

> **Pre-emptive mammography screening . . . at best, is a very mixed bag—it most likely causes more health problems than it solves.**

—H. Gilbert Welch, "Cancer Survivor or Victim of Overdiagnosis?," *Opinion Pages* (blog), *New York Times*, November 21, 2012. www.nytimes.com.

Welch is a professor of medicine at Dartmouth Institute for Health Policy and Clinical Practice.

....

Bracketed quotes indicate conflicting positions.

* Editor's Note: While the definition of a primary source can be narrowly or broadly defined, for the purposes of Compact Research, a primary source consists of: 1) results of original research presented by an organization or researcher; 2) eyewitness accounts of events, personal experience, or work experience; 3) first-person editorials offering pundits' opinions; 4) government officials presenting political plans and/or policies; 5) representatives of organizations presenting testimony or policy.

> **The bilateral mastectomy reduces [cancer] risk by 90 percent. Interestingly, it does not reduce the risk by 100 percent. Surgeons can't get every last breast cell.**

—Powel H. Brown, interviewed by Marc Silver, "Angelina Jolie's News: Docs Talk About Breast Cancer," *National Geographic*, May 15, 2013. http://news.nationalgeographic.com.

Brown is a breast medical oncologist and professor/chair of the Department of Clinical Cancer Prevention at the University of Texas MD Anderson Cancer Center.

....

> **No single medicine, procedure, or genetic test can guarantee that you won't develop breast cancer, since most breast cancers are NOT inherited.**

—American Cancer Society, "Breast Cancer Genetics: Is Testing an Option?," December 6, 2011. www.cancer.org.

The American Cancer Society is a nationwide, community-based volunteer health organization that is dedicated to eliminating cancer as a major health problem.

....

> **The issue of what women should do who are at higher risk of breast cancer due to a genetic mutation is fraught with complexities and difficult decisions.**

—National Breast Cancer Coalition, "Myth #20: With New Treatments, We Can Now Cure Breast Cancer," 2013. www.breastcancerdeadline2020.org.

The National Breast Cancer Coalition is a grassroots advocacy organization that is committed to improving public policies for breast cancer research, diagnosis, and treatment.

....

> **I look forward to the day when breast cancer appears in medical books under the chapter title, 'Cured Diseases.' Until then, let's take proactive steps to reduce risk where we can to save more lives (and breasts).**

—Lillie Shockney, foreword to *Fight Now: Eat & Live Proactively Against Breast Cancer*, by Aaron Tabor. Winston-Salem, NC: Aaron Tabor, 2010, Kindle edition.

Shockney, who has survived two bouts with breast cancer, is a University Distinguished Service Assistant Professor of Breast Cancer and administrative director of the Johns Hopkins Breast Center.

....

66 **Exercising four or more hours a week may decrease hormone levels and help lower breast cancer risk.** 99

—National Cancer Institute, "Breast Cancer Prevention," May 31, 2013. www.cancer.gov.

The NCI is the federal government's principal agency for cancer research and training.

66 **Treatment today is not much different from years ago. . . . Outcomes haven't drastically improved. We should be putting more dollars toward *preventing* breast cancer.** 99

—Margaret I. Cuomo, in Shaun Dreisbach, "7 Things No One Ever Tells You About Breast Cancer," *Glamour*, 2013. www.glamour.com.

Margaret I. Cuomo is a diagnostic radiologist in New York and the author of *A World Without Cancer*.

66 **Knowing the risk factors for breast cancer may help you take preventative measures to reduce the likelihood of developing the disease.** 99

—Cancer Treatment Centers of America, "Breast Cancer Risk Factors," 2013. ww2.cancercenter.com.

Cancer Treatment Centers of America is a national network of hospitals focusing on complex and advanced-stage cancer.

Can Breast Cancer Be Prevented?

- The American Institute for Cancer Research estimates that **38 percent** of all breast cancer cases in the United States could be prevented if people adopted simple lifestyle changes such as **healthier diets and more exercise**.

- The World Cancer Research Fund estimates that in the United States, **17 percent** of breast cancer cases could be prevented if people had a **healthy body weight**.

- According to the NCI, estrogen-only hormone therapy after menopause decreases the risk of breast cancer in women who have undergone a **hysterectomy**.

- The Mayo Clinic states that preventive medications known as **aromatase inhibitors** have shown promise in reducing the risk of breast cancer in women who are at high risk for the disease.

- Mehmet Oz, a cardiac surgeon and host of the popular *Dr. Oz Show*, states that moderate daily exercise reduces breast cancer risk by **15 to 25 percent**.

- According to the group Breastcancer.org, prophylactic breast surgery (removal of healthy breasts) may reduce a woman's risk of developing breast cancer by as much as **97 percent**.

Scant Funding for Breast Cancer Prevention

As part of a comprehensive review of breast cancer research, a federal advisory committee evaluated how several major government agencies were allocating research funding. One of these agencies was the US Department of Defense, which allocated $610 million in research funds between 2006 and 2010 for its Breast Cancer Research Program. Only 1 percent of that amount was allocated toward research that focused on prevention.

Distribution of US Department of Defense Breast Cancer Research Funding by Percent of Dollars Awarded for Fiscal Years 2006 to 2010

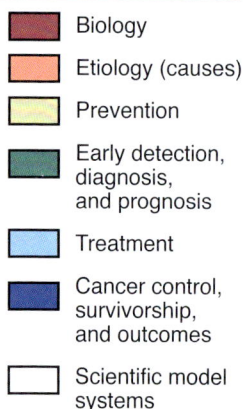

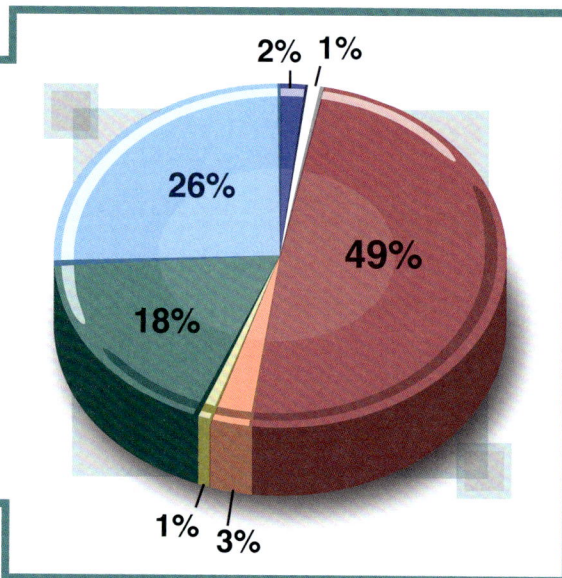

- Biology
- Etiology (causes)
- Prevention
- Early detection, diagnosis, and prognosis
- Treatment
- Cancer control, survivorship, and outcomes
- Scientific model systems

Source: Interagency Breast Cancer & Environmental Research Coordinating Committee, "Breast Cancer and the Environment: Prioritizing Prevention," February 2013. www.niehs.nih.gov.

- The NCI states that an antiestrogen drug called **tamoxifen** can lower the risk of breast cancer in women who are at high risk for the disease, and the effects last for several years after drug treatment has stopped.

The Mammography Controversy

Since the mid-1980s, the widely accepted medical standard for early breast cancer detection has been annual mammograms for women over the age of forty. In 2009 a US health task force disputed this established policy and made a controversial recommendation that mammograms start a decade later, at age fifty. According to a Harris poll conducted in April 2011, a majority of women disagree with the new recommendation.

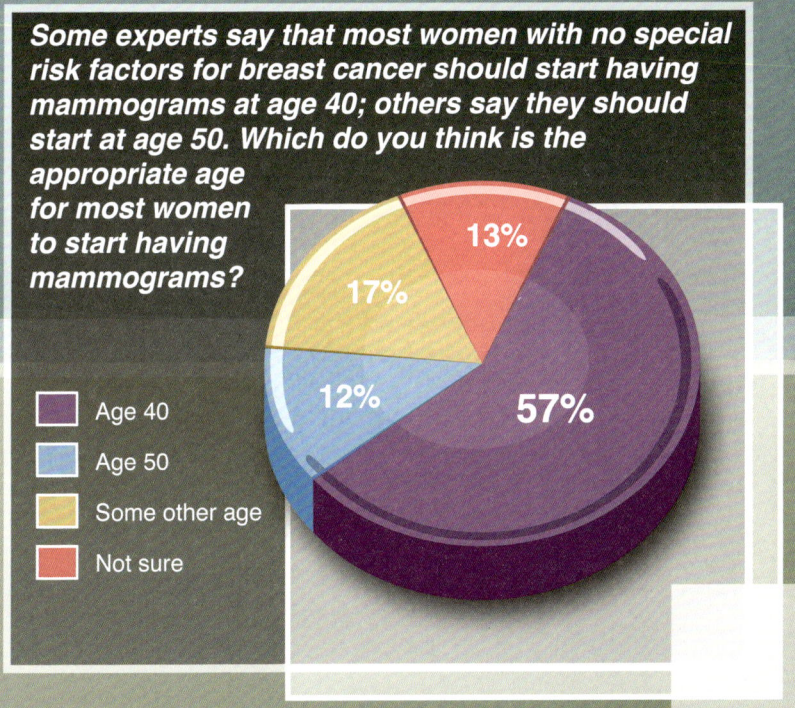

Some experts say that most women with no special risk factors for breast cancer should start having mammograms at age 40; others say they should start at age 50. Which do you think is the appropriate age for most women to start having mammograms?

- Age 40
- Age 50
- Some other age
- Not sure

13%

17%

12%

57%

Source: Harris Interactive, "Women in Their 40s Want Mammograms: Poll," May 4, 2011. www.harrisinteractive.com.

- According to Todd Tuttle, chief of surgical oncology at the University of Minnesota–Minneapolis, prior to 1980 fewer than **1 percent** of detected breast cancers were diagnosed as ductal carcinoma in situ (or stage 0); because of mammograms, the figure has risen to over **25 percent**.

When Genetic Testing Is Warranted

Genetic testing can detect the presence of a genetic mutation (such as in BRCA1 or BRCA2) that markedly increases the risk of developing breast cancer. Although it is a radical strategy, some otherwise healthy women who test positive for one of these mutations opt to have prophylactic mastectomies in an effort to prevent the development of breast cancer. This diagram shows the circumstances under which cancer experts say that genetic testing should be performed.

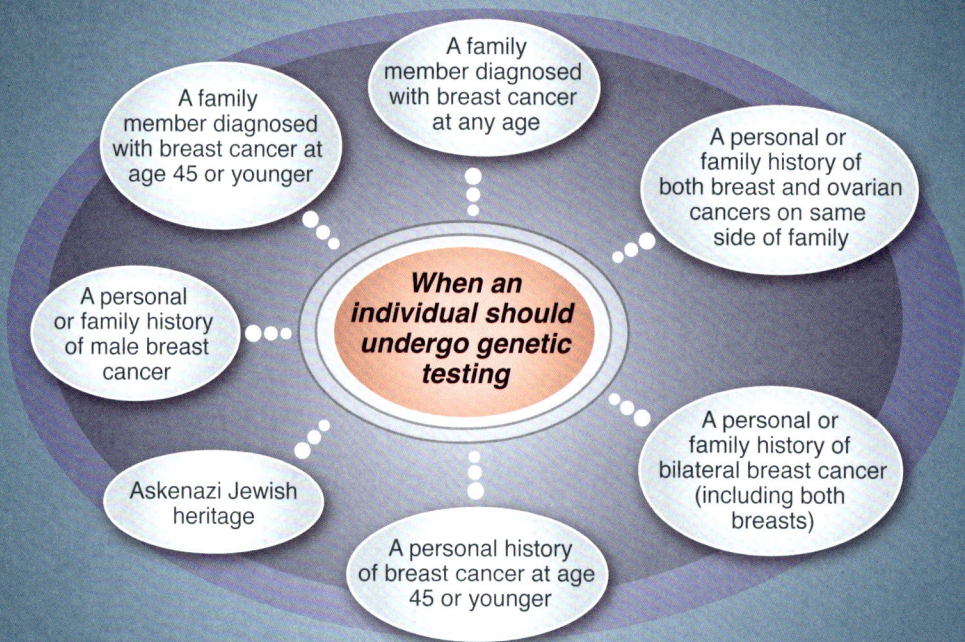

A family member diagnosed with breast cancer at any age

A family member diagnosed with breast cancer at age 45 or younger

A personal or family history of both breast and ovarian cancers on same side of family

A personal or family history of male breast cancer

When an individual should undergo genetic testing

A personal or family history of bilateral breast cancer (including both breasts)

Askenazi Jewish heritage

A personal history of breast cancer at age 45 or younger

Source: Susan G. Komen for the Cure, "What Is Genetic Testing for Breast Cancer and Who Should Get It?," *Komen Perspectives*, September 27, 2012, ww5.komen.org.

- A 2012 study funded by the World Cancer Research Fund revealed that women who increased their **dietary fiber** experienced a reduction in the risk of breast cancer.

- According to the group Breastcancer.org, women with abnormal BRCA1 or BRCA2 genes may reduce their risk of breast cancer by about **50 percent** by having prophylactic ovary removal before they start menopause.

- According to the NCI, when a type of vitamin A called **fenretinide** is given to premenopausal women with a history of breast cancer, it may lower their risk of developing a new breast cancer.

- Based on the findings of a University of Rochester (New York) Medical Center study published in May 2011, maintaining a sufficient level of **vitamin D** could be an important preventive measure against breast cancer.

- According to Mehmet Oz, a cardiac surgeon and host of the popular *Dr. Oz Show*, women who are over age sixty or who have a family history of breast cancer should consider taking an **estrogen-blocking drug**, which can stop breast cells from being affected by estrogen and lower the risk of breast cancer.

Key People and Advocacy Groups

American Cancer Society: A nationwide, community-based voluntary health organization that is dedicated to eliminating cancer as a major health problem.

Nancy G. Brinker: Originally from Peoria, Illinois, Brinker founded the Susan G. Komen Breast Cancer Foundation in honor of her only sister, Susan, who died of breast cancer in 1980 at age thirty-six. The organization was later renamed Susan G. Komen for the Cure.

Pierre Paul Broca: A nineteenth-century French surgeon and pathologist who was the first to describe inherited breast cancer in families in a systematic way. The BROCA genetic test that is widely used today was named after him.

Powel H. Brown: A noted cancer expert who is professor and chair of the Department of Clinical Cancer Prevention at the University of Texas MD Anderson Cancer Center in Houston.

George "Barney" Crile Jr.: An American surgeon who angered the medical establishment in the 1950s when he insisted that many women with breast cancer were being "mutilated" unnecessarily by undergoing radical mastectomies; he pioneered less radical forms of surgery, such as the partial mastectomy and lumpectomy.

Betty Ford: A former First Lady, Ford vastly helped increase awareness of breast cancer when she publicly acknowledged in 1974 that she suffered from the disease.

William Stewart Halsted: One of the founding physicians of Johns Hopkins Hospital who developed and performed the first radical mastectomy to treat breast cancer.

Angelina Jolie: An American actress and director who publicly announced in 2013 that she carries the mutated BRCA1 gene; because of that and her strong family history of breast cancer, she underwent a preventive double mastectomy.

Mary-Claire King: An American geneticist who discovered the BRCA1 gene in 1990.

Rose Kushner: A Washington, DC, journalist who was diagnosed with breast cancer in 1974 and who became an activist on behalf of other women with the disease; she urged women not to be afraid to challenge their physicians and to become better informed about the best treatment options.

Susan Love: A surgeon, breast cancer specialist, and patient advocate who in 1995 founded the research, education, and advocacy organization named after her.

National Breast Cancer Foundation: An organization whose mission is to save lives by increasing awareness of breast cancer through education and by providing mammograms for those in need.

National Cancer Institute (NCI): The federal government's principal agency for cancer research and training.

Albert Salomon: A German surgeon who in 1913 was the first to use X-ray technology to study breast cancer; his observations led to the use of mammography to diagnose the disease.

Susan G. Komen for the Cure: The world's largest grassroots network of breast cancer survivors and activists and a major fund-raising organization for breast cancer research.

Chronology

1838
German pathologist Johannes Müller demonstrates that cancer is made up of cells, although he erroneously believes that cancer cells do not come from normal cells.

1896
In an article published in the medical journal *Lancet*, Scottish surgeon George Beatson reports the first link between breast cancer and the female hormone estrogen.

1974
First Lady Betty Ford announces that she was diagnosed with breast cancer and underwent a radical mastectomy; within weeks of her announcement, thousands of women visit cancer screening centers across the United States.

1977
In performing the first full-body scan, American physician Raymond Damadian proves that the MRI technology that he developed is superior to X-rays for viewing the body's vital organs.

1850   **1900**   **1970**   **1990**

1865
German surgeon Karl Thiersch shows that cancers metastasize due to the spread of malignant cells, rather than through unidentified fluid as was previously believed.

1913
German surgeon Albert Salomon is the first to use X-ray technology to study breast cancer, and his observations lead to the use of mammography to diagnose the disease.

1975
The NCI reports that female breast cancer prevalence in the United States is 105 new cases diagnosed for every 100,000 women, and the mortality rate is 31 deaths for every 100,000 women.

1985
Research shows that a combination of lumpectomy and radiation therapy is as effective as total mastectomy.

1882
Renowned American surgeon William Stewart Halsted develops and performs the first radical mastectomy on a woman with breast cancer. The procedure involves removal of the breast, surrounding lymph nodes, and chest muscles.

1982
In memory of her sister who died of breast cancer, Nancy G. Brinker founds the Susan G. Komen Breast Cancer Foundation, which is later renamed Susan G. Komen for the Cure.

Chronology

1990
American geneticist Mary-Claire King discovers the BRCA1 gene and proves its link to breast cancer.

2013
Researchers from the University of California–San Diego School of Medicine identify a protein that appears to regulate the ability of cancer to metastasize.

1994
British researchers Michael Stratton and Richard Wooster discover the BRCA2 gene, which is linked to breast cancer.

2000
The US Congress passes the Breast Cancer and Cervical Cancer Prevention and Treatment Act, which provides greater access to cancer screening and treatment for low-income women.

2010
Researchers from the Institute of Cancer Research in the United Kingdom discover five genetic variants that increase the risk of developing breast cancer by about 16 percent.

1990 **2000** **2010**

1995
Surgeon and breast cancer specialist Susan Love founds a research, education, and advocacy organization called the Dr. Susan Love Research Foundation.

2006
The drug Herceptin is shown to reduce the risk of recurrence of HER2-positive breast cancer by more than 50 percent when used in a postoperative setting.

2011
Scientists at Penn State College of Medicine discover a virus that is capable of killing all grades of breast cancer within a week of first introduction in a laboratory setting.

1992
Self magazine releases its second National Breast Cancer Awareness Month issue and on the cover debuts the pink ribbon, a symbol that was chosen by philanthropist Evelyn Lauder and *Self* editor Alexandra Penney. Soon the ribbon becomes synonymous with breast cancer issues.

2012
In a *New England Journal of Medicine* article, researchers H. Gilbert Welch and Archie Bleyer describe a comprehensive study they conducted, that they say casts serious doubt on the benefits of using mammography to screen for breast cancer.

Related Organizations

American Association for Cancer Research (AACR)

615 Chestnut St., 17th Floor
Philadelphia, PA 19106-4404
phone: (215) 440-9300; toll-free: (866) 423-3965 • fax: (215) 440-9313
e-mail: aacr@aacr.org • website: www.aacr.org

The mission of the AACR is to prevent and cure cancer through research, education, communication, and collaboration. The search engine on its website produces a number of articles and fact sheets related to breast cancer.

American Cancer Society (ACS)

250 Williams St. NW
Atlanta, GA 30303
phone: (404) 320-3333; toll-free: (800) 227-2345
website: www.cancer.org

The American Cancer Society is a nationwide, community-based voluntary health organization that is dedicated to eliminating cancer as a major health problem. Its website offers a wealth of information about breast cancer, including fact sheets, videos, research findings, reports, and other publications.

Breast Cancer Fund

1388 Sutter St., Suite 400
San Francisco, CA 94109-5400
phone: (415) 346-8223; toll-free: (866) 760-8223 • fax: (415) 346-2975
e-mail: info@breastcancerfund.org • website: www.breastcancerfund.org

The Breast Cancer Fund works to prevent breast cancer by eliminating exposure to toxic chemicals and radiation that are linked to the disease. Its website offers information about which chemicals have been linked with breast cancer, how people can reduce their risk, research findings, a section called "Big-Picture Solutions," and a link to the Breast Cancer Fund blog.

Cancer Treatment Centers of America (CTCA)

1336 Basswood Rd.
Schaumburg, IL 60173
phone: (847) 342-7400 • toll-free: (800) 615-3055
website: ww2.cancercenter.com

Cancer Treatment Centers of America is a national network of hospitals focusing on complex and advanced-stage cancer. A number of informative publications and videos about breast cancer can be accessed through its website.

Dr. Susan Love Research Foundation

2811 Wilshire Blvd., Suite 500
Santa Monica, CA 90403
phone: (310) 828-0060; toll-free: (866) 569-0388 • fax: (310) 828-5403
e-mail: info@dslrf.org • website: http://dslrf.org

The Dr. Susan Love Research Foundation is dedicated to eradicating breast cancer and improving the quality of women's health through research, education, and advocacy. Its website offers a wide variety of information about breast cancer types, causes, survival rates, risk factors, treatment, and prevention. The site also links to the organization's blog.

Mayo Clinic

200 First St. SW
Rochester, MN 55905
phone: (507) 284-2511
website: www.mayoclinic.com

The Mayo Clinic is a world-renowned medical facility that is dedicated to patient care, education, and research. Its website has a search engine that produces numerous publications about types of breast cancer, the various stages, risk factors, and treatment options.

National Breast Cancer Coalition (NBCC)

1101 Seventeenth St. NW, Suite 1300
Washington, DC 20036
phone: (202) 296-7477; toll-free: (800) 622-2838 • fax: (202) 265-6854
website: www.breastcancerdeadline2020.org

The National Breast Cancer Coalition is a grassroots advocacy organization that is committed to improving public policies for breast cancer research, diagnosis, and treatment. Its website offers breast cancer fact sheets, a 2012 Progress Report, news articles, and a link to the group's blog.

National Breast Cancer Foundation (NBCF)

2600 Network Blvd., Suite 300
Frisco, TX 75034
phone: (972) 248-9200 • fax: (972) 248–6770
e-mail: info@nationalbreastcancer.org
website: www.nationalbreastcancer.org

The National Breast Cancer Foundation's mission is to save lives by increasing awareness of breast cancer through education and by providing mammograms for individuals in need. A wide variety of information is available through its website on breast cancer types, detection, diagnosis, and treatment, as well as myths about breast cancer and frequently asked questions.

National Cancer Institute (NCI)

NCI Office of Communications and Education
Public Inquiries Office
6116 Executive Blvd., Suite 3036A
Bethesda, MD 20892-8322
phone: (301) 496-1038; toll-free: (800) 422-6237
e-mail: cancergovstaff@mail.nih.gov • website: www.cancer.gov

An agency of the National Institutes of Health, the NCI is the US government's principal federal agency for cancer research and training. A wealth of information on breast cancer is available on its "Breast Cancer Home Page," which is accessible through the main website.

Susan G. Komen for the Cure

5005 Lyndon B. Johnson Fwy., Suite 250
Dallas, TX 75244
phone: (972) 855-1600; toll-free: (877) 465-6636
website: ww5.komen.org

Susan G. Komen for the Cure is the world's largest grassroots network of breast cancer survivors and activists and a major fund-raising organization for breast cancer research. Its website offers numerous informative publications about breast cancer as well as news releases, message boards, and a link to the organization's blog.

For Further Research

Books

Greg Anderson, *Breast Cancer: 50 Essential Things You Can Do*. San Francisco: Red Wheel/Weiser, 2011.

Edward Bauman and Helayne Waldman, *The Whole-Food Guide for Breast Cancer Survivors*. Oakland, CA: New Harbinger, 2012.

Margaret I. Cuomo, *A World Without Cancer*. New York: Rodale, 2012.

Samuel S. Epstein, *Stop Breast Cancer Before It Starts*. New York: Seven Stories, 2013.

Lynn C. Hartann and Charles L. Loprinzi, *The Mayo Clinic Breast Cancer Book*. Intercourse, PA: Good Books, 2012.

John S. Link, James Waisman, and Nancy Link, *The Breast Cancer Survival Manual*, 5th ed. New York: Holt, 2012.

Ruth O'Regan et al., eds. *Breast Cancer Journey*. Atlanta, GA: American Cancer Society, 2013.

Patricia Prijatel, *Surviving Triple-Negative Breast Cancer*. New York: Oxford University Press, 2013.

Laura Roppé, *Rocking the Pink: Finding Myself on the Other Side of Cancer*. Berkeley, CA: Seal, 2012.

Periodicals

Jenny Barnett, "Breast Cancer: Reduce Your Risk," *Harper's Bazaar*, October 2012.

Lisa Bernhard, "Too Young for Cancer," *Self*, October 2012.

Tara Brach, "Tap Into Your Power," *Prevention*, December 2012.

Lucy Danziger, "Be Fearless," *Self*, October 2012.

Shaun Dreisbach, "7 Things No One Ever Tells You About Breast Cancer," *Glamour*, October 2012.

Rory Evans, "Soul Survivor," *Allure*, October 2012.

Sunny Sea Gold, "The Best Thing I Would Never Wish on Anybody," *Redbook*, October 2012.

Heather Hurlock, "Happy Birthday, Pink Ribbon!," *Self*, October 2012.

Debra Huron, "The Courage to Look Beyond Breast Cancer," *Horizons*, Spring 2013.

Angelina Jolie, "My Medical Choice," *Opinion Pages, New York Times*, May 14, 2013.

Ed Kashi, "Mammograms: Who Needs Them?," *Prevention*, October 2012.

Jeffrey Kluger and Alice Park, "The Angelina Effect," *Time*, May 27, 2013.

Peggy Orenstein, "Our Feel-Good War on Breast Cancer," *New York Times*, April 25, 2013.

Bill Saporito, "Cancer Dream Teams: Road to a Cure?," *Time*, March 21, 2013.

John Sarkar, "Yes, We Men Get It Too!," *Men's Health* (India edition), October 2012.

Internet Sources

Breastcancer.org, "How Triple-Negative Breast Cancer Behaves and Looks," May 1, 2013. www.breastcancer.org/symptoms/diagnosis/trip_neg/behavior.

Cleveland Clinic, "Treatment Guide: Breast Cancer," 2012. http://my.clevelandclinic.org/Documents/cancer/breast-cancer-treatment-guide.pdf.

Jasen Lee, "Teen Recounts Journey Battling Breast Cancer," *Salt Lake City Deseret News*, October 31, 2012. www.deseretnews.com/article/865565752/Teen-recounts-journey-battling-breast-cancer.html.

Shari Rudavsky, "Young Breast Cancer Patients Fight a Lonely Battle," *USA Today*, October 7, 2011. http://usatoday30.usatoday.com/news/health/medical/health/medical/breastcancer/story/2011-10-04/Young-breast-cancer-patients-fight-a-lonely-battle/50655282/1.

Source Notes

Overview

1. Vanessa Bell Calloway, "Like Angelina Jolie, I Chose a Mastectomy for My Health," *Daily Beast*, May 28, 2013. www.thedailybeast.com.
2. Calloway, "Like Angelina Jolie, I Chose a Mastectomy for My Health."
3. Calloway, "Like Angelina Jolie, I Chose a Mastectomy for My Health."
4. Carey K. Anders and Nancy U. Lin, *100 Questions and Answers About Triple Negative Breast Cancer*. Burlington, MA: Jones & Bartlett, 2012, p. 2.
5. Johns Hopkins Medicine, "Breast Conserving Surgery." www.hopkinsmedicine.org.
6. Susan G. Komen for the Cure, "Chances for Survival Based on Cancer Stage," December 4, 2012. ww5.komen.org.
7. American Cancer Society, "Breast Cancer," February 26, 2013. www.cancer.org.
8. Breastcancer.org, "How Triple-Negative Breast Cancer Behaves and Looks," May 1, 2013. www.breastcancer.org.
9. American Cancer Society, "Cancer Prevalence: How Many People Have Cancer?," October 23, 2012. www.cancer.org.
10. Quoted in Fox News Detroit, "Inflammatory Breast Cancer: Unusual Symptoms Signaled a Problem," October 27, 2011. www.myfoxdetroit.com.
11. Fred Hutchinson Cancer Research Center, "Ashkenazi Jews and Cancer," 2013. www.fhcrc.org.
12. American Cancer Society, "Breast Cancer."
13. Mayo Clinic, "Breast Cancer," May 22, 2013. www.mayoclinic.com.
14. Mayo Clinic, "Breast Cancer."
15. National Breast Cancer Coalition, "Myth #20: With New Treatments, We Can Now Cure Breast Cancer," 2013. www.breastcancerdeadline2020.org.
16. National Breast Cancer Coalition, "Myth #20."
17. National Cancer Institute, "Breast Cancer Prevention," May 31, 2013. www.cancer.gov.

What Is Breast Cancer?

18. Quoted in Sue Thoms, "When Her Mom, Betty Ford, Had Breast Cancer: 'My World Collapsed,' Says Susan Ford Bales," MLive, April 9, 2013. www.mlive.com.
19. Nancy G. Brinker, "Thank You and Godspeed, Betty Ford," *Huffington Post*, July 15, 2011. www.huffingtonpost.com.
20. Metastatic Breast Cancer Network, "13 Facts Everyone Should Know About Metastatic Breast Cancer," 2013. http://mbcn.org.
21. Cancer Research UK, "How a Cancer Spreads," November 3, 2011. www.cancerresearchuk.org.
22. Cancer Research UK, "How a Cancer Spreads."
23. Kay Campbell, interviewed by Algerina Perna, "Courage and Strength: Living with Stage IV Breast Cancer," *Baltimore Sun*, January 15, 2013. http://darkroom.baltimoresun.com.
24. American Cancer Society, "Inflammatory Breast Cancer," August 30, 2012. www.cancer.org.
25. American Cancer Society, "Inflammatory Breast Cancer."
26. Quoted in James T. Mulder, "Woman Battles Rare, Aggressive Type of Breast Cancer

Often Misdiagnosed as Common Infection," Syracuse.com, January 8, 2013. www.syracuse.com.

27. Quoted in Mulder, "Woman Battles Rare, Aggressive Type of Breast Cancer Often Misdiagnosed as Common Infection."

28. Quoted in Shari Rudavsky, "Young Breast Cancer Patients Fight a Lonely Battle," *USA Today*, October 7, 2011. http://usatoday30.usatoday.com.

29. Quoted in Rudavsky, "Young Breast Cancer Patients Fight a Lonely Battle."

30. Thomas Sword, "My Story: Male Breast Cancer," Transforming Health, May 31, 2013. www.transforminghealth.org.

What Causes Breast Cancer?

31. Quoted in Stephanie M. Lee, "Breast Cancer Ties to Environment Probed," *San Francisco Chronicle*, February 26, 2013. www.sfgate.com.

32. Quoted in Jon R. Anderson, "Alarming Breast Cancer Rates Among Troops," *Marine Corps Times*, October 1, 2012. www.marinecorpstimes.com.

33. Quoted in Elisa Essner, "Fighting a Different Battle: Breast Cancer and the Military," Veterans United Military Spouse Central, October 30, 2012. www.veteransunited.com.

34. Breast Cancer Fund, "Which Chemicals Are Linked to Breast Cancer?," 2013. www.breastcancerfund.org.

35. Kangmin Zhu et al, "Cancer Incidence in the U.S. Military Population: Comparison with Rates from the SEER Program," *Cancer Epidemiology, Biomarkers & Prevention*, June 2009. http://cebp.aacrjournals.org.

36. Quoted in Jim Morris, "Study Finds Breast Cancer Risk for Women in Auto Plastics Factories," NBC News, November 19, 2012. http://investigations.nbcnews.com.

37. Breastcancer.org, "Genetics," June 13, 2013. www.breastcancer.org.

38. Fred Hutchinson Cancer Research Center, "Ashkenazi Jews and Cancer."

39. Quoted in Kate Johnson, "Breast Cancer Gene Mutations More Common in Black Women," Medscape, June 6, 2013. www.medscape.com.

40. Yuri Oiwa, "Study: 30% of Japanese Women with Family Breast Cancer History Have Genetic Mutation," *Asahi Shimbun*, June 3, 2013. http://ajw.asahi.com.

41. Garnet L. Anderson and Marian L. Neuhouser, "Obesity and the Risk for Premenopausal and Postmenopausal Breast Cancer," *Cancer Prevention Research*, April 2012. http://cancerpreventionresearch.aacrjournals.org.

42. Quoted in Brenda Goodman, "Obesity May Affect Breast Cancer Recovery," WebMD, August 27, 2012. www.webmd.com.

43. Quoted in Liz Szabo, "Report: More Research Needed on Breast Cancer, Environment," *USA Today*, December 7, 2011. http://usatoday30.usatoday.com.

How Successful Are Breast Cancer Treatments?

44. Quoted in Rachel McGrath, "Young Breast Cancer Survivors Ride for the Cause," *Ventura County Star* (Camarillo, CA), October 12, 2012. www.vcstar.com.

45. National Cancer Institute, "Adjuvant and Neoadjuvant Therapies for Breast Cancer," June 16, 2009. www.cancer.gov.

46. Paula Mitchell Joseph, interview with the author, June 20, 2013.

47. Joseph, interview.

48. Quoted in Brie Zeltner, "Copper Depletion Shows Early Success in Triple-Negative Breast Cancer: Discoveries," Cleveland.com, March 18, 2013. www.cleveland.com.

49. Breastcancer.org, "How Triple-Negative Breast Cancer Behaves and Looks."

50. Quoted in Weill Cornell Medical College, "Copper Depletion Therapy Keeps High-Risk Triple-Negative Breast Cancer at Bay," news release, February 13, 2013. http://weill.cornell.edu.

51. Quoted in Zeitner, "Copper Depletion Shows Early Success in Triple-Negative Breast Cancer."

52. Elaine Schattner, "How Well Do You Really Want to Know the Red Devil?," *Medical Lessons* (blog), December 11, 2009. www.medicallessons.net.

53. Quoted in Jane E. Brody, "For a Doctor, Survival and Transformation," *New York Times*, October 10, 2011. www.nytimes.com.

54. Quoted in Brody, "For a Doctor, Survival and Transformation."

55. Quoted in Brody, "For a Doctor, Survival and Transformation."

56. Kimberly Allison, "My Journey from Pathologist to Breast Cancer Survivor," Patient Power, Seattle Patient Care Alliance, September 14, 2011. www.seattlecca.org.

57. Quoted in Seth Robson, "Military Research Yields New Tool in Cancer Fight," *Stars and Stripes*, April 23, 2013. www.stripes.com.

58. Quoted in Robson, "Military Research Yields New Tool in Cancer Fight."

Can Breast Cancer Be Prevented?

59. Interagency Breast Cancer & Environmental Research Coordinating Committee, *Breast Cancer and the Environment: Prioritizing Prevention*, National Institute of Environmental Health Sciences, February 2013, p. 1-2. www.niehs.nih.gov/about/assets/docs/ibcercc_full_508.pdf.

60. Interagency Breast Cancer & Environmental Research Coordinating Committee, *Breast Cancer and the Environment: Prioritizing Prevention*, p. 1-2.

61. Lillie Shockney, foreword to *Fight Now: Eat & Live Proactively Against Breast Cancer*, by Aaron Tabor. Winston-Salem, NC: Aaron Tabor, 2010, Kindle edition.

62. Quoted in Stephanie Eckelkamp, "Eat to Beat Breast Cancer," *Prevention*, April 2013. www.prevention.com.

63. Quoted in Stephanie Cary, "YSC Tour de Pink, 3-Day Bike Race to Help Women with Breast Cancer," *Los Angeles Daily News*, October 3, 2012. www.dailynews.com.

64. Quoted in Jason Kane, "Commentary: Why Mammograms Are So Crucial," *PBS Newshour*, December 25, 2012. www.pbs.org.

65. Quoted in Kane, "Commentary: Why Mammograms Are So Crucial."

66. H. Gilbert Welch, "Cancer Survivor or Victim of Overdiagnosis?," *New York Times*, November 21, 2012. www.nytimes.com.

67. Welch, "Cancer Survivor or Victim of Overdiagnosis?"

68. Quoted in Kane, "Commentary."

69. Angelina Jolie, "My Medical Choice," *Opinion Pages, New York Times*, May 14, 2013. www.nytimes.com.

70. Quoted in Diane Mapes, "Like Sharon Osbourne, More Women Getting Preventive Mastectomies," *Today*, November 5, 2012. www.today.com.

71. Quoted in Mapes, "Like Sharon Osbourne, More Women Getting Preventive Mastectomies."

72. Quoted in Lidia Dinkova, "Opening Up the Conversation About BRCA Genetic Testing," *Miami Herald*, June 30, 2013. www.miamiherald.com.

73. Johns Hopkins Medicine, "Frequently Asked Questions About Genetic Testing." www.hopkinsmedicine.org.

74. Johns Hopkins Medicine, "Frequently Asked Questions About Genetic Testing."

List of Illustrations

Index

Note: Boldface page numbers indicate illustrations.

About the Author

Peggy J. Parks holds a bachelor of science degree from Aquinas College in Grand Rapids, Michigan, where she graduated magna cum laude. An author who has written more than one hundred educational books for children and young adults, Parks lives in Muskegon, Michigan, a town that she says inspires her writing because of its location on the shores of Lake Michigan.